Charlotte heard the communal gasp and felt as though it had escaped from her own body. She saw Bitsy, the society gossip columnist, writing furiously before a camera flashed in her eyes.

"*Impending* marriage?" someone asked.

"Accomplished," her stepmother corrected.

"To whom?" another guest asked eagerly.

Her stepmother had been so convincing, that even Charlotte waited for an answer. But there was no groom. . . .

Prepared to die of humiliation, Charlotte was shocked when she felt a strong male presence behind her. An arm came around her and pulled her close. Warm, dry lips pressed a kiss to her temple.

"Ladies and gentlemen," the male voice said, "may I present Mrs. Derek Cabot."

Dear Reader,

American Romance's tenth-anniversary celebration continues....

For the past three months, we've been bringing you some of your favorite authors, and some brand-new ones, in exciting promotions. In its decade, American Romance has launched the careers of over forty writers and made stars of a dozen more.

Muriel Jensen is one of them. It's *her* tenth anniversary, too. She sold her very first book to American Romance and has gone on to write seventeen more for the series.

A native of Massachusetts, Muriel now lives in Astoria, Oregon, with her husband who is also a writer, two calico cats and a malamute named Deadline. She has three grown children.

We hope you've enjoyed our special tenth-anniversary selections. And we look forward to many more anniversaries of success....

Sincerely,

Debra Matteucci
Senior Editor & Editorial Coordinator

MURIEL JENSEN

THE UNEXPECTED GROOM

Harlequin Books

TORONTO • NEW YORK • LONDON
AMSTERDAM • PARIS • SYDNEY • HAMBURG
STOCKHOLM • ATHENS • TOKYO • MILAN
MADRID • WARSAW • BUDAPEST • AUCKLAND

Published October 1993

ISBN 0-373-16507-2

THE UNEXPECTED GROOM

Chapter One

"My life sounds like the plot line of a soap opera."
Charlotte Morreaux, alone in her classic white Duesenberg, reviewed her current situation as she drove
through the wooded canyon northeast of Los Angeles.

"Wealthy heiress falls in love with up-and-coming
corporate executive in her father's company. Executive leaves heiress standing at the altar. While heiress
begins life anew by leaving father's employ to open
specialty wedding shop, executive falls in love with
daughter of heiress's father's partner. No problem.
Heiress number one holds no grudges. However, heiress number two's mother does. She dislikes heiress
number one and is always finding innovative ways to
embarrass her."

"Charlotte, you *have* to help me!" Kendra Farnsworth had pleaded the day before on the telephone.
"My wedding dress is a horrid monstrosity! Please
bring a selection of dresses from Borrowed Magic to
the shower Sunday afternoon. I'd much rather have
one of your vintage dresses than this . . . this thing!"

Charlotte heard the rustle of taffeta in the background and guessed that the offending dress had been shoved aside.

But I wasn't coming to the shower, Charlotte said to herself. There isn't enough money or power or amaretto truffles in the whole world to make me....

"Bitsy Tate's coming," Kendra added in all apparent innocence. In reality, the announcement had the same effect as holding a French cannon to Charlotte's temple. "I told her I was calling on you to save my wedding."

Bitsy, who wrote Bitsy's Tidbits for the *Times,* had made her gossip column's reputation on Charlotte's embarrassing abandonment at the church the year before. As a reporter, Bitsy was brutally honest and thorough. Nothing escaped her attention—or her column. As a woman, she leaned toward viciousness—and she was a friend of Elizabeth Farnsworth, Kendra's mother.

"She thinks it's all very poetic," Kendra went on in her breathless ingenue voice.

Charlotte smiled to herself. It *was* poetic. Like something from the pen of Ogden Nash.

"Of course I'll come," she'd replied with forced enthusiasm. "I have a few things you might like."

She was already imagining an 1890s gown with a pinaforelike front that would enhance Kendra's blond fragility. Charlotte Morreaux might look poetic and tragic in front of Bitsy Tate, but Borrowed Magic would be brilliant.

With a sigh of resignation, Charlotte turned onto the back road to her father's estate. It would help, she told herself bracingly, that the shower was being held on her home turf. Kendra's father and Charlotte's father had been partners in the ever-booming field of high technology since their daughters had been children. Both men appeared completely ignorant of the antagonism that existed among the Morreaux and Farnsworth women.

Charlotte liked Kendra. Though Charlotte was oldest by three years, and though the girls were very different in interests and attitude, they'd managed to get along when their fathers' alliance forced them together throughout their childhood and teen years.

Their mothers hadn't fared as well. Elizabeth's standard for selecting friends was a complicated equation of ancestry, social status and bank balance. While Edward Morreaux held the latter with a vengeance, he was the son of a North Dakota farmer and chose his friends for their intelligence and their ability to sit still while he explained his current project in great detail.

Caroline, Charlotte's stepmother, traced her roots to one of the signers of the Declaration of Independence, but she had no pretensions whatsoever. And she didn't mind prodding those who did.

What resulted between her and Elizabeth was a kind of creative one-upmanship that had carried through the years.

Charlotte was smiling over thoughts of her father and Caroline when she saw the other car. It came at her from the side road, a low-flying blur of red.

Startled sharply to awareness, she turned out of its way as two sets of brakes screamed. She was flung forward and then back as metal crunched and glass shattered. The Duesenberg shuddered and then settled, her scream and the reverberations of the crash pulsing around her like a bad aura. Then all was silent.

She blinked, wondering what had happened, when her door was yanked open.

"Charlie? Charlie!" A concerned voice shouted in her ear as hands grasped her shoulders, then ranged clinically down her arms and over her ribs. A grazing touch over the tip of her breast penetrated her shocked disorientation.

She turned vaguely to the source of the noise and focused on a very familiar face.

"Oh, no," she groaned. "Not you. Not today."

Bourbon-brown eyes glanced up from a hands-on examination of her legs. Then Derek Cabot fixed a devastating smile on her. "I'm afraid so, Charlie. How've you been?"

His fingertips dipped under her knees and swung her legs around as he nudged the car door aside with his shoulder. "Stand up. Let's see if you're okay."

She tried to shake his hands off. "I'm fine."

"I'd like to see for myself."

Charlotte gave him the Duchess of Winter look. Though it had been a year since she'd left the company, Derek thought of her often, and he always thought of her in her persona of titled gentry.

He took hold of her wrist and pulled her to her feet. "Your patrician glare doesn't frighten me, remember?'' he said, frowning at her, then putting a diagnostic hand to her forehead. ''You look a little disoriented. Do you feel dizzy?''

''Yes,'' she admitted, batting his hand away. ''Seeing you always upsets me. What are you doing here?''

''I was invited to the shower.''

That seemed to annoy her. ''Why?''

He put his hands in the pockets of his brown slacks and leaned his weight on one leg. ''There are people who like having me around. I'm sorry if that upsets you.''

She rotated a stiff shoulder muscle. ''My dismay at seeing you is purely chemistry. I don't like you. Aaagh!'' She had turned as she spoke and noticed for the first time the accordion-pleated front fender of her classic car now permanently affixed to the trunk of a fragrant eucalyptus.

She went to it, like a mother to an injured child. ''Look what you did to my Duesie!''

''What *I* did?'' he replied defensively, coming up behind her. ''When you're driving something older than you are, you should slow down at intersections.''

She rounded on him, her long, straight blond hair flying out like a banner, her pale iris-colored eyes giving him that look calculated to make him feel like a peasant.

''It is *not* an intersection—it is a lazy country driveway crossed by a rural road! Who does sixty down a curving rural road?''

"I do," he replied. "I have places to go. Unlike some people who are content to dawdle along as though time will stop for them."

She huffed impatiently. "Oh, God. Let's not have that argument again. This is a wedding shower, not a power meeting."

Derek reached into the dash of his Porsche for his cellular phone. He'd forgotten, he thought, waiting for someone at the garage to pick up, how much he enjoyed being shouted at by her. He always had, which was a good thing, because that was the way they'd exchanged most information when they'd worked together—at the tops of their voices. Opposite work styles had made dealing with each other almost impossible. Still, he was enough of a scrapper to feel that the relationship would have possibilities in another setting.

"Canyon Car Care."

"Les, it's Derek." He winked at Charlotte as she approached him, frowning. Apparently she didn't like him taking over resolution of the accident. Too bad. "I just hit a classic Duesenberg. A '31?" he asked her.

"Thirty-two," she corrected. "La Grande Phaeton."

He repeated the information to Les. "Right side's a mess. Front fender's crunched against the tire. Can you pick it up on a flatbed? I don't want it towed."

"Right away."

"Good." He gave him the location. "The owner and I are already late for a party, but I'll be by the shop this afternoon."

"How's the Porsche?" Les asked.

"Perfect," he answered. "She hit a tree, not me."

"Lucky break."

As Derek leaned into the car to replace the receiver, Charlotte folded her arms—another gesture of the Duchess of Winter. She looked as though she were considering the disposition of an unruly serf.

"I might have wanted my car taken to my own garage," she said.

He straightened away from the car and acknowledged that possibility with a nod. "But Canyon Car Care is the best. He works on a Daimler and a Bentley that I've seen there from time to time. And my insurance company's used to dealing with them."

She raised a wheat-colored eyebrow. "Then you do admit responsibility for the collision?"

He couldn't deny it. He'd been going too fast, spotted the Duesenberg, knew who had to be driving and, for one critical split second, let his mind wander from the road to the woman.

"Yes," he said. "I do. Come on. I'll drive you up the lane. We'll send one of your father's men back to stay with your car until Les picks it up."

She studied him dispassionately for a moment, then turned and went to the left rear door of her car.

He watched her move with interest. For a woman who carried herself like untouchable royalty, she had the most seductive tush he'd ever had the pleasure to observe—it was just a little too round, with the most enticing sway in the snug skirt of the teal forties-era suit. He'd often thought of it as stamped with a royal crest.

"No hat today, Duchess?" he asked, forcing himself to think about something else.

She pulled three deep, wide boxes out of the back and placed them in his arms. The Borrowed Magic gold-on-white logo glinted in the early-afternoon sunlight of the southern California fall.

Then she reached in again and emerged with a picture hat the same color as her suit. She placed it on her head at an elegant angle.

She followed him to the convertible, rearranged the boxes when he placed them in the back, then allowed him to seat her and close her door.

But she looked a little disconsolate when he slid in behind the wheel. He thought he knew why. He'd taken Caroline to the Children's Hospital Ball the night before when Edward had been waylaid by a long-distance call at the last moment.

"I understand one of the dresses you've brought is going to save the wedding of the decade," he said.

She glanced his way in surprise. "How did you know?"

"Caroline told me. It's generous of you to come through for Kendra," Derek said. "Considering the circumstances."

Charlotte drew in several deep breaths, trying to relax. "Actually, I'm not that big. I'm thinking of it as business. Borrowed Magic is obliging a client, not I."

"No good," he said. "You *are* Borrowed Magic."

"Please." Her voice was a little high. "I'm having enough trouble bracing myself to face everyone as it is. Why don't you just pull up in back and we'll go in through the kit—"

But he was already driving around the colonnaded front of the plantation-style house. A stately row of liquidambar trees just showing tips of red lined the circular drive.

A white-coated young man came to open Charlotte's door while another opened Derek's and took the keys from him.

"Is this the weekend I get to take the Porsche to the beach, Mr. Cabot?" the boy joked.

"Funny, Naldo. I need a favor." Derek explained about the accident. "Will you go keep an eye on it for Miss Morreaux?"

Naldo grinned at Charlotte. "Anything for Miss Morreaux. I'll take care of it."

"A duchess doesn't go in through the kitchen," Derek said, taking Charlotte's elbow and asking the second attendant to bring in the boxes. "And, anyway, you once lived here. You belong here."

"Every man and woman in there," she said quietly as they crossed the broad veranda, "knows that Trey Prentiss literally left me at the altar."

He looked down at her as though her dilemma confused him. "Then it seems to me *he* should be the one embarrassed, not you."

She closed her eyes to summon patience. "Yeah, well, it doesn't work that way. All anyone knows is that Trey is handsome and brilliant and that I must have done something pretty awful to have scared him away like that at the last minute. Particularly since he's obviously willing to head for the altar again with someone else.''

''That's because marrying Kendra doesn't take any guts. Marrying you would.'' He pushed a spot between her shoulder blades that made her stiffen her spine. ''Come on. Let's have the wintry royal smile. When you do that, you always look as though nothing touches you and nothing matters to you. People admire someone who can remain above the struggle.''

She wasn't sure she liked that assessment of herself, but the door opened at that moment, and Plowright, the Morreauxs' butler, gave them a broad smile and swept them inside.

Caroline was upon them immediately, plump and fragrant and exuding the warm generosity that had made her and Charlotte fast friends. Though Charlotte had been prepared to resent her when her father had brought her home, Caroline had filled the dark, lonely void with a wonderful sweetness coupled with an innocent and often hilarious propensity for causing trouble. She'd been the best friend Charlotte had ever had.

Charlotte was taken in a silky embrace, then held at arm's length and studied with a concerned green gaze.

''Are you all right?'' she asked softly.

''I'm fine,'' Charlotte assured her with more bravado than she felt. ''Unfortunately my car isn't. Derek just made a Japanese fan of it.''

Derek smiled as Caroline embraced him. "She exaggerates. Two months with a good body-and-fender man and a small fortune, and the Duesenberg will be good as new."

"Meanwhile," Charlotte said, "I'll be getting around Los Angeles on roller blades."

"Char—lie!" The throaty cry came from beyond the foyer and halfway across the gray-and-rose living room where the shower guests were congregated.

Every one of the hundred or so heads turned in Charlotte's direction. She would have given her entire seven-figure inheritance to be somewhere on a mountaintop in Tennessee.

Kendra, slender and doll-like in red wool, remained standing in the middle of the living room, arms extended toward Charlotte so that Charlotte was forced to walk the gamut of guests and go to her, or appear the vengeful woman scorned, the sore loser. She went.

"Kendra," she said graciously, injecting her voice with warmth. "I'm happy for you." She saw a flare of light as a camera flash lit the scene. Over Kendra's shoulder, she saw Bitsy Tate taking notes, and Darby Grant, the photographer who worked with her, sighting through his lens for another shot.

Charlotte pulled away and added quietly, "The dresses are in the foyer."

"*Won*derful." Kendra reached a hand out for Trey, who stood just beyond them. "I can try them on here after the shower and you can tell me what you think. You won't *believe* the mess Jean Michel designed for me."

Jean Michel was one of the West Coast's most sought-after designers. Charlotte couldn't imagine that he'd created a monstrosity. Kendra had always had a flair for drama.

"Darling." Kendra drew Trey closer. It was the first time Charlotte had seen him since her own wedding rehearsal. She squared her shoulders and smiled.

"Please," Kendra said to Trey. "Thank Charlotte for saving the day for us."

Charlotte had always thought Trey Prentiss resembled Mark Harmon with his boyish yet jaded smile. He seemed even more handsome at that moment, taller, blonder, more charming.

He gave Charlotte a sheepish, self-deprecating grin as he extended a hand toward her. "Hi, Charlie," he said. "It was good of you to do this for us, considering . . . well, I mean after I . . ."

She'd have found it very satisfying to simply stand there until he finished the sentence—" . . . after I made a fool of you and myself." But she knew every ear in the room was listening and she simply couldn't be that cruel.

She put her hand in his. "Happy to do it," she said, her voice firm and convincing. "Borrowed Magic promises you a beautiful bride."

"Well, there you are!" Edward Morreaux's voice boomed in Charlotte's ear and she turned gratefully for her father's bear hug. "Hear you and Derek 'bumped into each other' on the lane." He laughed at his clichéd joke. "Bound to happen. *He's* always in a hurry, and *you* never know where you're going." He shook his head, smiling, as though he considered that an amusing situation.

He took two glasses of champagne from the tray of a passing waiter, handed her one and put the other in Derek's hand as he approached.

Kendra and Trey wandered away and conversation began to buzz again.

Edward beamed at his daughter. "Damned if you aren't turning out to be an entrepreneur in your own right. Everywhere I turn, someone's telling me about someone they know who bought or rented a dress from your shop, or had you design their wedding. I guess you were wasted all those years as head of public relations for Morreaux–Farnsworth."

Charlotte cast a glance at Derek. "Funny that we didn't notice it until Derek came along." She smiled at the man in question, her expression carefully neutral. "If you hadn't put him in charge of my department, we might still think I was doing a good job."

"Your work was always late," Derek pointed out quietly.

"I was trying to do it well."

"The requirements of PR are often very immediate. You were too much of a dreamer."

"Now that's all water under the bridge," Edward said placatingly. "It all worked out for the best. You left to do your own thing, Charlie, and you're happy, and our news releases are getting out on time. *I'm* happy."

"Charlotte, darling!" Elizabeth Farnsworth, tall and elegant in a silky café-au-lait designer suit, took

Charlotte in her famous touchless embrace where lips never met cheek. "You're looking well," she pronounced with what must appear to everyone else to be auntlike affection. Only Charlotte saw the dislike in her eyes. "What's new with you?"

Politely, Charlotte began a brief résumé of the past few months, the shop next door into which she'd expanded, the accessories she'd added.

"No," Elizabeth said softly, maliciously. "I mean, what's new in your love life?" Then she added with a deepening of that suspect smile. "A few more years, darling, and you'll be thirty. It's time to make plans."

Charlotte was torn. She could shock everyone by telling Elizabeth it was none of her business. She could make up a wild tale about a Turkish prince, or she could admit that she hadn't been on a date in a year, that she hadn't wished herself home in front of the television after the first hour. But she had an image to maintain for her business.

She opened her mouth, prepared with a tactful reply, when Caroline appeared at her shoulder and said loudly, cheerfully, "Go ahead and tell them, Charlie."

The simple sentence with its suggestion of mystery reverberated through the room. People who had wandered into the parlor or out into the foyer wandered back. Edward looked up from a discussion with several of his golf buddies. Trey and Kendra, nuzzling in a corner, turned in her direction.

Charlotte had a well-developed sense of self-preservation. And it had grown even stronger over the past year. The obvious question was, "Tell them what?'' but a significant look in her stepmother's eyes prevented her from asking it.

Elizabeth, however, did it for her. "Tell them what?''

Charlotte felt gooseflesh rise on her arms when her stepmother smiled and giggled. That was always a prelude to trouble. It meant she had a plan. And every plan she'd ever had meant disaster for someone.

"Well . . .'' Caroline put a hand to the back of Charlotte's waist and smiled at her guests who were pressing closer. "I'm afraid Kendra and Trey have to share the festivities this afternoon. Charlotte has come home not only to see that Kendra has the perfect wedding dress . . .'' She sent a benevolent smile in Kendra's direction. Then she turned it on Charlotte. "But to announce her marriage.''

Charlotte heard the communal gasp and felt as though it had escaped from her own body. Marriage! Oh, God. Soap opera plot line number two! Out of the corner of her eye she could see Bitsy writing. A flash lit the side of her face. Elizabeth appeared to be suffering a spasm at the prospect of the spotlight being stolen from her daughter.

"Impending . . . marriage?'' Elizabeth asked.

"Accomplished,'' Caroline corrected with obvious satisfaction.

There were more gasps, more exclamations.

"To whom?'' Elizabeth asked in a demanding tone.

Even Charlotte waited for the answer. Caroline had been so convincing thus far, she felt sure her stepmother must have a reply.

She obviously didn't. Thus was the nature of Caroline's disasters. An ingenuous innocence carried her so far, then abandoned her. In defense of her stepdaughter, she'd tried to put Elizabeth Farnsworth in her place by showing her that, despite the past, Charlotte was as capable of finding a husband as Kendra was. She simply hadn't thought the scenario through. She hadn't cast the part of the groom.

Prepared to die of humiliation in front of these people yet again, Charlotte was shocked when a strong male voice behind her said with convincing firmness, "To me."

An arm came around her and pulled her close. Warm, dry lips pressed a kiss to her temple. "Ladies and gentlemen," the voice said. "May I present Mrs. Derek Cabot?"

Chapter Two

Cameras flashed again as the crowd moved in with squeals of delight and congratulations.

"What," Charlotte demanded of Derek under her breath while smiling at friends and neighbors, "are you doing?"

"I've no idea," he replied, an arm still around her while he reached the other out to shake Caleb Farnsworth's hand. "Caroline looked like she needed help."

Edward caught his daughter's eye from across the room. His expression was apologetic but resigned. He glanced at his wife fielding questions from the excited guests and shook his head with the same loving tolerance he'd shown for the past eleven years. He gave Charlotte an almost imperceptible shrug that reminded her that he never knew what to do about Caroline, either. She'd get no help from that quarter.

"Well, isn't this rather sudden?" Elizabeth asked, her eyes filled with calculating suspicion. "I mean, word was Charlotte quit the company when Edward brought Derek back from the New York office because they couldn't get along."

Caroline, radiant with Derek's rescue, shrugged grandly and laughed. "Well, you know how it is with sparks. Sometimes you get a fire, and sometimes you just get beautiful fireworks." She glanced at Charlotte and Derek and winked.

"When did you get married?" Elizabeth insisted.

"While I was on a business trip." Derek replied with the smallest hesitation that might have been mistaken for a moment taken to enjoy the memory. He squeezed Charlotte and gave her an intimate look that suggested they shared the memory. "I asked her to join me and we decided it would be nice to travel together forever."

"How romantic!" someone gushed.

Charlotte was afraid to breathe. Deception was not her strong suit, and getting involved in an intrigue with Caroline held terrifying prospects. An intrigue that involved Caroline *and* Derek was too awful to contemplate.

"I think we should..." she began, planning to make a clean breast of everything.

"Toast the newlyweds," Caroline interrupted with a sweep of her elegantly braceleted arm. "Excellent idea. Plowright, more champagne, please."

"Caroline, you can't..." Charlotte began, prepared to confront her, in front of everyone if necessary, to stop this silly charade.

Caroline turned to her with the same smile that had once proven to the teenage Charlotte that, though her stepmother was her friend, she was no pushover. It had preceded a month's grounding and loss of car privileges.

"Don't tell me I can't, darling," she said under her breath. "That always makes me crazy. You know that. Just follow Derek's lead. He's doing beautifully."

"He's lying!" Charlotte whispered harshly. *"You're lying."*

Caroline rolled her eyes. "Don't be tedious, Charlie. We have Liz Farnsworth on the run and I'm not giving up the chase for anything."

"Relax," Derek said in her ear. "Here comes the champagne."

She turned to look up into his dark brown eyes, now alive with amusement, and said urgently, "Derek, everyone will tell everyone else. Tomorrow it'll be in Bitsy's column."

He did not seem concerned. "In a few days interest will wane and the whole thing will die a natural death. The important thing right now is not to embarrass your parents."

"You're going to be pretty embarrassed when everyone discovers you lied."

Plowright served the champagne himself. Derek accepted a glass from him and a second for Charlotte. "Nothing embarrasses me," he said. "That's the up side of not giving a damn what people think of you. Now get it together. You're supposed to look like a radiant bride."

When everyone was holding a champagne glass, Caroline smiled up at her husband, who had come across the room to join her.

"I think this is a job for the father of the bride," she said. Her eyes were filled with unrepentant deviltry.

Charlotte saw him return the look with a promise of retribution. But when he looked out at his friends, his smile appeared genuine, his manner one of the delighted, indulgent parent.

"To surprises," he said, a little edge of irony in his voice that made Charlotte and Caroline exchange a look. "To the little everyday charms that make love develop where you would least expect to find it..." He turned to Charlotte with a look that told her something she couldn't quite grasp. "To the magic that makes it all work, that takes two very different human beings and makes them one loving unit." His eyes went from Charlotte to Derek. "To Mr. and Mrs. Cabot."

Charlotte stared at her father while everyone else drank. Where had that come from? For an impromptu toast delivered on the heels of a phony announcement, his words had been touching and, by all appearances, heartfelt.

"Drink," Derek urged softly. "Elizabeth's watching."

Charlotte downed her champagne, not out of obedience, but out of a desperate need to feel the alcohol warm her stomach. It was threatening to revolt.

She was grateful when attention finally turned back to Kendra and Trey. Everyone found chairs or made themselves comfortable on the floor while the couple opened presents.

Charlotte tried to lose herself in a corner, but Bitsy made a point of relinquishing her chair in the middle of the room.

"Oh, please don't..." Charlotte tried to protest, but Bitsy was adamant—and expectant.

"I need to be moving around," she insisted. She looked from one to the other and asked with veiled suspicion, "Is this one of those business-decision marriages? A merger of stocks rather than hearts?"

For an instant Charlotte didn't know what to say. The temerity of the press often astounded her. Then she knew what it would take to get Bitsy off their backs, at least for the duration of the afternoon.

She looked up at Derek, barely made eye contact while wondering how to get her thought across to him, when he showed her that he understood completely.

With one hand, he swept her hat off, with the other he circled her waist, pulled her to him and made everyone around them, including Bitsy, gasp when he looked down into Charlotte's eyes. Even a *Forbes* magazine reporter could not have mistaken the look for business.

Then he lowered his head and opened his mouth over hers.

It's an act, Charlotte told herself. That made it easier to play her part. It also made her realize that if what she felt was make-believe, she had the potential to play Hamlet.

She was instantly, completely seduced. His tongue invaded her mouth—to demonstrate their passion for each other to their audience, she was sure—but it did its work with a tender finesse that astonished and excited her.

His hand in her hair held her still as he went a little deeper, probed a little farther, then flattened his other hand against her back until her breasts, through the gabardine suit and the leaf-lace bra beneath it, were spread against the wool-blend houndstooth of his jacket.

Her eyes closed, her brain turned to oatmeal by the surprise, she experienced the embrace with all the sensual detail she'd have known had they been naked.

A little frisson of sensation rippled up the center of her being and made her tremble in his arms.

When he raised his head, it was a moment before she could open her eyes. When she did, she was aware first of the conflicting emotions in his. She saw triumph, a trace of shock and the unmistakable arrogance of a man who knows he's made a woman respond to him.

Then she became aware of the silence and remembered where she was. Color flooded her face.

Derek straightened her with a hand between her shoulder blades and grinned at Bitsy.

"Yes," he replied. "Definitely a business-decision marriage." He sat in the chair and pulled Charlotte down into his lap and patted her hip. "I've always loved her bottom line."

Everyone laughed except Bitsy, who looked him in the eye and told him without words that he might be a business genius, but she was also extremely gifted—at ferreting out the truth. That he may have fooled everyone else, but she suspected there was more to this marriage than met the eye.

Then she raised her glass, offered her congratulations, then left them as Kendra and Trey began to open their opulent packages.

"Oh, God," Charlotte exclaimed under her breath. "She doesn't believe us."

"She doesn't want to believe us," he corrected quietly, resting his forearm familiarly across her knees. "But I think that's because, deep inside, we convinced her."

"That doesn't make sense. Why would she *not* want to believe us?"

"If your livelihood depended upon scandal," he pointed out reasonably, "would you want to believe we were really happily married? She'd have much better copy if she could convince everyone you were broken-hearted over Trey, or that your stepmother had perpetrated a sham marriage to show up the Farnsworths."

"That's what she did."

"I know, but do you want all of greater Los Angeles to know it?"

"Oh, God." Charlotte thought that over and decided the best thing she could do for all of them was disappear.

She tried to stand, but Derek held her in place. "Where you going?" he whispered.

"Moscow," she replied, pushing against him. "It's free now. I'll change my name, make a new start..."

He looped his arms around her waist and laced his fingers to keep her there. "We've got this under control. Just relax and trust me. You're the romantic, remember? Doesn't this feel just a little like you're caught in a fairy tale?''

She hooked an arm around his neck and smiled because she noticed Bitsy's photographer poised for a shot in their direction. ''It feels a little like I'm in a bad nightmare. And it's all your fault!''

''You seem to be forgetting Caroline's involvement.''

''Caroline would have been forced to admit she was lying if you hadn't stepped nobly forward and declared yourself my husband.''

He frowned at her seriously. ''You'd have preferred that? Caroline humiliated and you still a spinster?''

''I *am* still a spinster. Although I prefer using 'career woman.' It's just the poor people we've deceived who think of me as a bride.'' Then she sighed as she came to terms with the other half of his question. ''Of course I don't want Caroline humiliated, but she can't just create her own reality like that.''

''She did it for you.''

''I know that,'' she said impatiently, ''but look at the mess she's made. Tomorrow someone, probably me, is going to have to tell the press it was all a joke.''

''Why?''

''Because it isn't true!''

He frowned at her again, careful to do it with a loverlike indulgence for the sake of all the glances that continued to wander their way. ''For a woman who wrote press releases that sounded like novels, and embroidered the facts until they were barely recognizable, you've taken a very pedantic turn. Can't you just relax and play the game?"

"Marriage is not a game," she said stiffly, practically.

"How do you know?" he countered. "You ever been married?"

"No," she replied patiently, "but if I were, I wouldn't think of it as a game."

"Maybe that's why most marriages don't last," he suggested as the crowd oohed and aahed over a pasta maker. "They forget to play."

"The point," she said, "is that we've deceived people."

"Oh, I don't know." He became suddenly grave. "I always thought we could have had a relationship under different circumstances. That kiss made me sure of it."

There had been something there. Something she'd never experienced before, even with the man she'd been about to marry.

She averted her eyes and pretended to study the crowd. "We were acting. That wasn't real."

"We were acting," he said, "like a man and a woman with something important to say to each other."

She had felt that. But she didn't want to. She turned a lavender-gray gaze on him. "We said all we had to say to each other the day I quit."

"That was business," he said. "I'm talking about life. Love. Sex."

"I don't want those with you," she said brutally.

But it was like striking armor with a whiffle ball. He didn't seem to notice.

"That's not what your lips told me."

"If you don't stop talking about this," she said in a stern undertone, "I'm going to scream, slap your face and march indignantly out of here and let everyone in the room think whatever they like."

"And you would give Bitsy material for days."

That was true, but Charlotte chose not to think about it. She concentrated her attention on Kendra and Trey, ignoring Derek as much as was possible considering she was sitting in his lap.

It wasn't long before the procession around the room of towels and cappuccino makers and health spa certificates began to blur. She snapped her eyes open several times, thinking that she shouldn't have drunk the second glass of champagne when she'd had only three hours' sleep the night before worrying about this afternoon.

Then a firm, warm hand began to rub wide, relaxing circles up her spine and the blur slipped away into darkness, taking her with it.

DEREK HAD ALWAYS wondered what it would be like to hold Charlotte. Of course, he'd always imagined her awake when he considered it, but accepted that having her asleep at the moment was probably better. Awake, she'd have never stayed.

But now the crowd had thinned. Edward, Caleb, Trey and a few others were playing poker in the den, and Caroline, Elizabeth and Kendra were upstairs with the dresses Charlotte had brought.

The room where he sat had been darkened and the furniture left strewn around in deference to the sleeping duchess in his arms. Caroline had whispered that it could all be put to rights in the morning, then had winked at him conspiratorially when she left the room.

She considered him part of her deception because he'd come to her rescue. Ordinarily that might have made him nervous. He's seen her in action before.

But this was not an ordinary situation. He had Charlotte Morreaux in his arms. It was difficult for him to think about anything else.

As he studied Charlotte's eyelashes, the thinly mascaraed silky fans fluttered open.

Her head came off his shoulder abruptly and she looked around at the darkened room empty of people.

"What happened? What time is it?" she asked, her body tense with confusion. His hands were loosely clasped around her and he freed one to steady her back.

"We were caught in a time warp," he replied, "this is our living room on the planet Uranus, and the year is 2457."

She turned to him with a perplexed look. Then, because she was still sleepy and probably because they were alone and her guard had slipped, she smiled at him.

"Why do we have so many chairs?"

"Because on Uranus," he answered, straight-faced, "women are fertile twenty-two days of the month and gestation is only four months long. We have—" he did a quick perusal of the room "—thirty-seven children."

She giggled and settled back against him.

That was a nice surprise, he thought. She awoke with a sense of humor. He valued that in a woman.

"Where are they all?"

"Ah...on the road. We have a basketball team, a rock group, a construction company and an all-female marching band. They're supporting us in our old age."

She giggled again, and after a moment of silence he felt her deep sigh. He enjoyed the moment. Soon enough she would remember what had happened, remember that she disliked him intensely.

"I've always wanted four boys," she said, her tone dreamily conversational. "And a place on a stream where they could build a raft and pretend to be pirates."

It was easy to take the fantasy on another turn. "Sort of a Tom Sawyer–Peter Pan fusion. I don't know. That encourages play. How would they support us with a little raft?"

"Oh..." Her eyelashes fluttered against his jaw as she considered. A strange weakness invaded his body. "They could carry freight," she said, "transmit regular weather reports and set out lobster pots."

"That could work. But I don't think we have lobsters on Uranus."

"We're back in L.A."

"We don't have lobsters in L.A., Charlie."

She was quiet a moment, then she sat up slowly. "Well, that's always been the trouble with dreams. In reality, you can never fit them into your life." She gave him a curiously bittersweet smile and tried to stand.

"Hey." He held her down with a gentle hand on her arm. "I haven't found that to be true. I've always dreamed of holding you and . . . here we are."

She leaned an elbow on his shoulder and looked into his eyes, her expression still soft with sleep and the leftover raft scenario. Strands of her blond hair fell on his jacket. "This isn't a dream, Cabot," she said softly. "It's a lie."

"There's not that much difference between the two," he said, reaching up to tuck the hair back behind her ear, needing an excuse to touch it. "A dream is something that exists only in your mind. In most cases, a lie is just a creative interpretation of what is. In either case, it would probably just require a little work on the subject's part to make the dream a reality and the lie a truth."

She stared at him a moment, succumbed to a smile, then just as quickly frowned. "You have a scary brain, Cabot."

"Charlie!" Caroline exclaimed, flipping on the living room light. The shadowy little haven dissolved. "I'm glad you're awake. Elizabeth has the most wonderful idea."

Caroline's faintly concerned tone didn't support the words. Elizabeth smiled down at Charlotte and Derek.

Charlotte settled back against her pseudo groom, partly for the sake of the sham she didn't seem able to elude, and partly because Elizabeth's cold smile suggested the tangle was about to draw even more tightly around her, and the solidity of Derek's chest was very comforting.

"Really?" she asked. "What is that?"

"Kendra's in love with all the dresses you've brought," Elizabeth said, "but I think she'll be deciding on the Victorian with the choker neckline and the wide frills on the shoulder."

Charlotte nodded. The pinafore dress. She had known it would be perfect.

"Trouble is," Elizabeth went on, "the mood of everything else is out of sync—the bridesmaids' dresses, the flowers, the centerpieces for the reception."

Since she didn't look particularly displeased about the fact, Charlotte waited.

"Kendra and Caleb and I have talked it over and decided the best solution would be to hire you to make the changes, to have you as a guest at our home next week to help us do what's necessary to get everything done at the last minute. Money's no object, of course."

A week with Elizabeth? Desperation took hold of her. "But you'll be entertaining the wedding party," she said calmly. "You'll have your family from out of town..."

Elizabeth shrugged. "But we have so much room." She sank gracefully into the chair opposite them and smiled with pretended empathy. "Since you're such newlyweds, I wouldn't dream of separating you. I thought you could stay in the smaller of the two guest houses so you can have some time together. The press will be staying in the bigger one.''

Charlotte tried not to show terror. She knew the Farnsworth estate well. The two little guest houses behind the big house sat on opposite sides of the rose garden, but shared a common lane to and from the house. And the house the press would share had a picture window; it would be impossible for anyone in the other house to make a move without being seen. She suspected Bitsy would be watching her and Derek every moment.

To her relief, Derek demurred before she had to. ''I'm sorry,'' he said sincerely, ''but I'm in the middle of Farnsworth–Morreaux's plans to acquire Windsor Tech. I wouldn't have the time...''

''Nonsense!'' Caleb Farnsworth came into the room, followed by Charlotte's father. ''Elizabeth has so many plans for me next week, I won't be able to come into the office, but if you were on hand to meet with me when I had a moment, and if Edward were to join us, we could go over Windsor Tech's notes and work the points into our contract.''

''Excellent idea.'' Edward was quick to agree. ''We could get some serious work done free of the everyday office crises.'' He clapped Caleb on the back and grinned at Derek. ''It'll be almost as good as a hunting trip.''

Elizabeth blinked; Caroline looked up at Edward with a pitying look. Charlotte thought he might not be that far wrong—she was beginning to feel like an exhausted prey about to be run to ground.

Charlotte turned pleading eyes on Derek, lost for a believable excuse. He simply raised both eyebrows with an innocence that belied the pull at his bottom lip.

"Well, we never did have time for a honeymoon," he said. "What do you think?"

Artful, she thought. He'd put it back on her. She couldn't refuse the invitation without looking unwilling to help and probably bitter over Trey. And she also couldn't refuse for Derek's sake when the partners who employed him obviously thought the situation ideal.

Before Charlotte could answer, Kendra's head peered around the corner of the hallway. On it was a coronet of crystal-beaded flowers and leaves. Yards of netting hung from it to the floor.

"Is Trey gone?" she whispered.

"Yes," Elizabeth replied. "But he made me promise to have you call him after dinner."

"Oh, good." Kendra, flushed and radiant, emerged from the corridor. The slim-fitting white satin bodice was beautifully accented by a wide flounce of lace that trimmed the shoulders and crossed her breasts to meet at the waist and make it appear even narrower than it already was. A diaphanous skirt contributed to the fragile look of the bride.

Kendra did a turn in the middle of the room, obviously waiting for praise.

"You're breathtaking, Kennie," Caleb said.

"It is beautiful," Caroline agreed softly.

Elizabeth reminded, as though she couldn't help herself, "It is borrowed, darling. Are you sure?"

"I'm sure," Kendra said firmly. Then she went to kneel in a riffle of white near Derek and Charlotte's chair. "But now we have to fix everything else. You will come and help me, won't you? There'll be so much to do! We have to do something about my attendants' dresses, and I was just going to have calla lillies, but now that will never do. Please, Charlotte. You *have* to help me."

Charlotte wanted desperately not to do this, but she was able to relate to Kendra's dilemma on a curiously unselfish level. This was Kendra's wedding day, and just because her own had been botched, she wasn't unsympathetic to Kendra's wish that hers be perfect. It should be every woman's right. And it was Borrowed Magic's job.

"Of course I will," she said, and for a moment Derek almost had both women in his lap.

As Kendra scurried off, Bitsy Tate wandered out of the kitchen, stirring coffee in a china cup.

Charlotte started, unaware that the reporter had remained behind when everyone else had left.

As though reading her mind, Bitsy glanced her way as she sipped, then put the cup in its saucer and smiled slowly. "Well, I had to see how it all turned out, didn't I? This is a lovely little drama. Guaranteed to be front page of the section. So you will be staying with the Farnsworths even though you haven't even had time for a honeymoon yet?"

Charlotte accepted that she was in an indefensible position. Surrender was her only option. But she wouldn't forget who had helped put her there, and she vowed to see that it would be as difficult for him as it would be for her.

She gave Derek a seductive smile and traced her index finger tauntingly over his bottom lip, deciding that paybacks could start now. "Every moment we're together is like being on a sunny tropical beach. Isn't it, darling?"

He nipped the tip of her finger and made her yelp and withdraw it. Then he smiled wickedly into her eyes. "Paradise," he concurred. "When do we move in?"

Elizabeth studied them a moment, then smiled stiffly and replied, "Tomorrow morning. Then you'll be on hand to meet everyone at lunch."

"There's no reason Edward and I have to be there," Caroline tried to withdraw gracefully. "We're just a few miles away. If you need us, we can be there..."

"Now, now," Elizabeth insisted. "Our home is half again as big as this." She gave a quick look around that seemed to suggest the Morreauxs' four thousand square feet simply wasn't adequate. "There's plenty of room. And you can help me with my mother. She wants to spend all her time in the kitchen and I can't spare the pounds." Another eloquent glance suggested that Caroline's weight was a lost cause already. "Well, Caleb. Let's round up our daughter and be on our way."

Everyone gathered at the door as the Farnsworths took their leave. Derek hooked a familiar arm around Charlotte's shoulder, ignoring her warning glare.

Elizabeth dispensed her touchless hugs and thanked Caroline and Edward for hosting the shower. "It was so thoughtful of you. Kendra's into quaint little things these days and it was all so appropriate.''

Caleb and Edward seemed to notice no undercurrent in the politely spoken thank-you. Caroline ignored it, a veteran of many years of Elizabeth's social tyranny.

Charlotte barely resisted administering a good shove into the potted geraniums.

The moment the door closed on the Farnsworths, Charlotte turned on Caroline.

"Caroline, what in the name of heaven have you done?" she demanded, confronting her under the gleaming chandelier.

Caroline returned glare for glare. "Well, good heavens, girl. Someone had to step in for you! Elizabeth asks you what's new, obviously to put you on the spot, and you launch into a business report!"

"At least that was honest!" Charlotte retorted. "Caro, you lied to a house full of people and members of the press! Tomorrow it'll be in the *Times* that Derek and I are married!"

"Charlie, don't shout at her," Edward said, putting a protective arm around his wife's shoulders. "I'm sure Caroline meant well."

"Dad..." Charlotte made a conscious effort to lower her voice. "Tomorrow Derek and I have to move into their guest house and live there together for a week until the wedding. In case you've forgotten, we are not married. We don't even like each other."

Edward failed to look properly horrified. Instead he smiled at Derek. "Good save, son. I did think Caro was dead in the water there for a minute."

"Good save?" Charlotte repeated incredulously. "Good save! He made it worse! He confirmed the lie!"

Edward rolled his eyes and patted her shoulder, like one would a child having a tantrum. "Charlie, you get so upset about the strangest things. Think of what this whole thing will do for your business. When everyone sees Kendra in that dress, they'll all come flocking to you for vintage dresses. Everyone will want a wedding like hers."

"And when Bitsy Tate puts her hand to this," Derek added, "she'll have you so smothered in wistful romance, sheer stardust will bring all the dreamy young girls to you. The jilted bride who nobly saved her ex-fiancé's wedding."

Caroline smiled slowly. "They'll say you were able to do it because you've found love at last with a handsome devil who came up the hard way and won your heart."

Charlotte put a hand to her stomach. "I'm going to be sick."

"You're going to be famous," Caroline corrected.

Chapter Three

"I'll take the side by the door," Derek said, following Charlotte into the guest-house bedroom.

Charlotte took one look at the pink-and-white flowered wallpaper, the eyelet bedspread and the half-dozen lace-trimmed pillows stacked against the wicker headboard and quickly turned around. She collided soundly with the chest of Derek's tweedy jacket.

"You can have both sides," she said, pushing past him and back into the small oystershell-and-green living room. She dropped her makeup case, her suitcase and her suit bag in the middle of the floor and went into the small, corridor kitchen.

"And where are you going to sleep?" Derek leaned a shoulder in the kitchen doorway and watched her fill a kettle shaped and painted like a fish. "The bathtub's stylish but very uncomfortable looking."

"I'll sleep on the sofa." The kettle on, she opened cupboards looking for a cup. She found a complete set of blue pedestal pottery mugs.

"It doesn't open," he said.

"Not a problem." She instituted another search for tea bags, instant coffee, anything. "I don't move in my sleep."

"I sleepwalk," he said. "You won't be any safer in the living room than you'd be beside me."

She cast him a glower that told him what she thought of his attempt to lighten the mood. It couldn't be done. She'd awakened without a sense of humor this morning. He'd driven her home the night before, after stopping by the garage to assure her that her beloved Duesenberg was being well cared for. When they'd parted company, she'd been resigned if not happy with the prospect of the week ahead.

This morning, living a week in this little house with the press on one side and the Farnsworths on the other seemed impossible. She couldn't do it.

Derek took several steps into the narrow room. "What's happened since last night?" he asked quietly.

She pried at the top of a square tin of tea. When she couldn't budge it, she said impatiently, "Seems like nothing around here opens."

He reached a long arm out, took the tin from her and opened it effortlessly.

"You haven't answered my question," he reminded her as he handed the tin back.

"Want a cup?" she asked. "It's—" she studied the product name so she wouldn't have to look at him or answer him "—a delicate blend of oolong and orange pekoe."

"I would love a cup," he said, reaching into the cupboard where she'd gotten a mug and pulling down another. "I'd also like an answer."

Cornered, she unwrapped two tea bags and pretended to think. "Well, let's see. I packed a few things, took a shower, brushed my teeth, had my nightly cocoa and pretzels and went to bed with the latest Regency novel."

"Most amusing," he said, opening the door on the small refrigerator and peering inside. "That unwillingness to be open is the same quality that made you so difficult to work with."

She spun toward him, hands on her hips. "*I* was not difficult to work with. *You* were difficult to work with. You wanted to boss everything about me, not just my job."

"That isn't true. You're just so spoiled and stubborn you take every suggestion as a criticism."

"You tried to tell me who...whom...to date!"

He interrupted his perusal of the contents of the refrigerator to throw her a grin. "And I was right, wasn't I? Prentiss turned out to be a jerk."

"He isn't a jerk," Charlotte corrected righteously, "he's a coward. There's a difference."

"Not in my book."

"At Farnsworth–Morreaux, I may have had to work by your book. In my life, I did not."

"So you ran away."

"I quit."

"Same thing."

"Not in *my* book."

He pulled out a clear square box of blueberry muffins and placed it on the counter. "Your book was written so long ago, no one's heard of it. Your book was probably originally taken down on papyrus. Your book is just like *you*—beautiful and romantic but entirely impractical."

"I believe in facts carefully researched, skillfully assembled and tastefully distributed. Until you came to F and M, that was not considered a crime."

He opened the cupboard again and pulled down plates.

"I don't want a muffin," she said.

He replaced a plate and opened the refrigerator in search of butter.

"Why do you think your father put me in charge of your department?" he asked. "Because it was weeks behind and Prince Prentiss wasn't doing anything about it. He was apparently afraid of you at work as well as in bed."

Charlotte swatted him with a handy towel. "How dare you say a thing like that! How dare you express an opinion on a subject you know nothing about!"

He gave her a glance she couldn't read, then neatly pulled the head off a muffin and buttered it. "You haven't been well loved," he said. "I can see it in your eyes. And if he'd really taken you over the top, it'd show in his. And it doesn't."

"Oh, right. Like sexual experience is a visible thing."

"It is. It's subtle, but it's there."

The kettle whistled. Charlotte snapped off the burner and lifted the three clear glass bubbles at the fish's mouth to pour. Derek held first one tea bag while she poured, then the other.

"Trey wasn't afraid of me," Charlotte insisted, consciously controlling her tone, wondering why a few minutes in Derek Cabot's company always had her shouting. "He just believed in letting me do my own work in my own way."

"Which resulted in it not getting accomplished."

"Why can't you admit," she said, lifting her cup and placing her other hand protectively under it, "that you just never liked me?" And she marched out of the kitchen to the living room.

Derek popped the last bite of muffin into his mouth and followed her, wondering how a smart woman could be so dense.

"My personal feelings had nothing to do with it," he said. And the moment the words were out of his mouth, he knew they'd been a mistake. They echoed in the small, stylish little room like the lie they were—only not for the reason she thought.

"You didn't want me there," she said, putting her cup on the glass-topped coffee table and sitting in the middle of the green polished cotton sofa, "because you decided even before you knew me that I was the spoiled, stubborn daughter of the boss who'd gotten her job on relationship and not on merit, and you couldn't stand that because no one's ever given you anything. You've had to fight for it. So you had to fight me."

He put his cup beside hers and pulled off his jacket, thinking that she was absolutely right. He'd felt precisely that way—and he'd been right. She'd taken the job because her father wanted her near him, and she'd done adequately when the company had been smaller.

But recently, acquisitions and diversity of product had happened with a swiftness that required a PR department that could act as quickly. It had taken him only days to see that Charlotte's relaxed, carefully attentive style couldn't cope.

She was already dressing like a woman from another time, and her locker and her desk drawers were filled with fashion accessories that looked like artifacts to him. She talked continually about one day opening her own shop.

The morning they locked horns over the production delay of a sales brochure, because her promotional copy hadn't been ready, had given her that opportunity.

What she'd never understood was that their mutual antagonism was based on more than their different work styles. Her closeness made him edgy. When he was near, she became defensive. He thought it was time he found out what it was all about.

"Actually, I liked having you around," he admitted easily as he tossed his jacket on the rocker at a right angle to the sofa. "I just knew you should be doing something else. Anyway..." He sat in a corner of the sofa and squared one leg on the other. "We shouldn't be talking about the office. We're supposed to be on our honeymoon." He grinned wickedly. "We're supposed to turn this into that sunny, tropical paradise you told the Farnsworths about."

She edged over one cushion, noting unhappily that the sofa was squishy. One night on it and she'd probably have to wear a back brace for the next month.

"I was just playing the role."

"And very well. All you have to do is keep it up for a week and we're home free."

She sipped tea, then thought she should explain her position in no uncertain terms. "I'm only doing this because I wouldn't hurt my parents for the world..."

"I understand."

"And Borrowed Magic is just beginning to take off. I can't afford any bad press right now."

"Of course not."

She sighed dramatically at his amenable acquiescence. "You needn't patronize me."

He turned to face her, setting his cup on the table and frowning. "Do you have to take issue with everything? I was simply agreeing with you. I also don't want to see Ed or Caroline get hurt, and bad press is a bad thing. Ease up, will you? If you keep up this attitude, everyone will wonder what I saw in you."

"No, they won't. It's considered very strategic to marry the boss's daughter." Still, she knew he was anything but an opportunist—at least in that respect. He'd never once done anything anyone might have construed as an attempt to reach her father through her. In fact, he'd found it more expedient to get her out of the way. She had to ask. "Why are *you* doing this?"

He reached to the table for his cup and took a sip before answering.

"Your father reminds me of mine," he said, thoughtfully resting his cup on his bent knee. "Only mine died too young to see all his big ideas grow."

That surprised her. She'd never thought of him in relation to a family. He seemed so solitary. "What did your father do?"

"He sold and repaired small appliances," Derek replied, a fond smile on his lips as he absently turned his cup. "He had a shop in Salem, Oregon, and another in Corvallis. He was always going to move into a mall, open a big furniture store and put his repair shop in the back, but he was always too busy to stop and put a deal together." The smile faded suddenly and he took another sip of tea. "He had a fatal heart attack when I was a sophomore in high school."

Charlotte was a little shaken by that information—Derek Cabot loved his father and missed him.

"And," he went on, the past gone from his eyes, the future alight in them, "I couldn't resist the temptation to satisfy my curiosity about you."

She blinked at him. "Curiosity about what?"

"About whether or not you would remain the Duchess of Winter in my arms and in my bed."

"The Duch . . . who?"

"The Duchess of Winter," he replied, putting his cup down again. "You know, that imperious woman you always become when you want to put someone off." He mimicked her raised eyebrow, her cold glance, then, comically, the dismissing toss of her head.

"Of course that doesn't work as well if you don't have this long veil of blond hair, but you know what I mean."

"I do not!" she denied, a giggle just below the surface of her indignation. His interpretation of her behavior had more humor in it than criticism. "I don't do that."

"Please," he said. "You do one of the three all the time. You have a few other signature moves I could never duplicate, so I didn't try. Are you afraid if you find a man who makes your heart pound your dignity might slip?"

"Of course not." She replied with the same glance she'd just denied using. "Nothing could make my dignity slip."

"Oh . . ." he said slowly, studying her with serious intent. "That's almost too much of a challenge to walk around. Do you want to test that?"

Trepidation filled her. And a subtle excitement. But she was off men at the moment and she'd never been one to flirt with danger or tempt the fates.

"Thanks, but it was tested a year ago when I walked up the aisle and there was no one there to meet me." She made herself look directly into his eyes. "I was bloody, but unbowed. And so I shall remain."

"Bruised and stiff. That about describes you." He reached a hand along the back of the sofa and ran a fingertip across her cheekbone. "That's got to be uncomfortable. I'll bet I could buckle your knees."

He saw her eyes widen. She thought so, too? Well. Wasn't life full of the damnedest surprises.

"That would make me fall," she pointed out primly.

"I would be there to catch you," he explained. "That's the whole point."

"You know," she said, at a loss to answer him and needing a way out of the conversation, "you worry a subject to death. Forget it. I am quite happy the way I am, thank you." She glanced at her watch and stood. "We should be changing for lunch."

"Changing what?"

"Clothes." She looked down at her fashionable silk sweats. "I'm going to put on a dress."

He unfolded slowly to his feet. "Do people still do that? I thought changing for meals was something people did only in the movies about high society."

"Yeah, well, this is the Farnsworth estate," she said, throwing her dress bag over the back of a chair and rummaging through it. "Elizabeth sleeps with the social register under her pillow. And we seem to be living the *Philadelphia Story*. I keep thinking the director will come through any moment and shout, 'That's a wrap. Take ten, people.'"

"Drama's good for the soul." Derek picked up his bag and headed for the bathroom. "You can have the bedroom," he said over his shoulder. "Change in there. I'll sleep on the sofa, but I should probably leave my bag in the bedroom so we don't raise the suspicions of anyone dropping by."

"I will be happy to sleep on the sofa," Charlotte insisted nobly.

"Well, I *would* enjoy your company." Derek smirked from the bathroom doorway.

She straightened, a Victorian floral print clutched against her, to frown at him in exasperation. "I meant, while you were in the bed."

He pretended surprise. "Oh. Here I thought I was going to get to buckle your knees, after all. Take the bed," he said, pushing the door closed to end the discussion.

EVERY NERVE ENDING in her body was dancing. Charlotte tilted her head sideways to brush her hair, then swung her head to settle it against her back. She tied it at the nape of her neck with a thin black ribbon.

The little tremor raced along under her skin, a curious sensation she didn't recall experiencing before. Nerves? she wondered. No. She was no stranger to deadlines and stress. She'd supervised enough weddings in the year she'd been in business to learn how to cope.

This was different. This was personal.

Big surprise, she told herself, smoothing the lace collar that sat neatly on the romantic rose print of her cinch-waisted dress. You're living a lie with a man who seems determined to unsettle you. This is nerves with a vengeance.

But she knew it wasn't. The moment she opened the door and spotted Derek standing in the middle of the small living room, a fresh blue shirt under the tweedy jacket, she knew it was... awareness. Sexual awareness.

Good, she told herself ironically. You're required to give the performance of a lifetime over the next six days or humiliate your parents and kiss your business goodbye, and you're experiencing runaway estrogen.

Derek extended an arm toward her as she approached. She was just about to slap it away and tell him to keep his theatrical attentions for the benefit of their audience when she realized they did indeed have one.

Bitsy Tate sat in the rocker, a white high-heeled sandal on the oystershell-colored carpeting propelling her gently back and forth.

"Bitsy thought we might as well walk to the big house together," he said.

Charlotte slipped smoothly into his arm, a sweet smile in place. "Are we in danger of being unable to find it ourselves?" she asked.

"I just thought when you're looking into each other's eyes all the time," Bitsy said, standing and shouldering her bag, "you often miss the obvious. But I could give you a head start, if you'd prefer."

"We'd be delighted to have you join us," Derek said, offering his free arm. "Mornings, we love company. Nights, we like to be left alone."

At the door, he stepped out from between the women to open it and usher them through. As Charlotte passed him, following Bitsy, he asked loudly enough for the reporter to hear, "Did you find my keys?"

Charlotte understood the question was intended to assure Bitsy they were sharing the room. She decided the best part about acting was the opportunity to improvise.

"They were under the dresser," she said. "Must have happened when you cartwheeled off the bed. Ow!"

His pinch of retribution was swift and stinging. Bitsy, fortunately, seemed to take it as newlywed play.

KENDRA'S TWO ATTENDANTS had also arrived that morning, one a little redhead from Houston, and the other a Harvard-accented Bostonian with yards of curly dark hair. Kendra explained that they'd been college friends and met in Gstaad every winter and Cozumel every summer. Charlotte had been surprised when she'd first learned Kendra would have only two attendants. She'd imagined she'd want half a dozen beautiful young women streaming up the aisle.

"Of course, that'll stop now." A bright little woman in a boldly patterned muumuu and sneakers with white socks wandered into the palatial, vaulted-ceiling living room where Kendra was making introductions. She put a floury hand around Kendra's waist, oblivious to the expensive crepe fabric of her dress. "Now you'll have to stay home with your man and raise babies."

"Mother," Elizabeth said with strained patience, pulling the woman's arms from around her daughter, "we just got that dress at Susanna's. I thought you were helping in the kitchen."

"I was," the woman replied cheerfully, "but I thought it was only polite to come out and greet my granddaughter's friends."

Elizabeth tried to turn her back toward the kitchen. "Well, we're just about to..."

"Chow down. I know, I'm fixing it." Elizabeth's mother pulled deftly away from her and turned to study the new arrivals with interest. "Hope you like this stuff. It's quiche. Looks a little insipid to me. I thought a good hearty stew would have been nice, but you know Lizzie. Gotta watch her gut."

She backhanded Elizabeth's midsection with a hearty laugh. Elizabeth doubled over and Caleb steadied her with a distinctive twitch to his lip.

Charlotte had to take action or burst into laughter. She extended her hand for a floury handshake.

"I'm so pleased to meet you," she said. "I'm Charlotte Mo—" She stopped herself just in time, giving an apologetic smile around the room. "Cabot. Charlotte Cabot," she said. "I'm a newlywed. I keep forgetting I'm not a Morreaux anymore."

"I'm Babs McGuffy." Elizabeth's mother shook Charlotte's hand, then looked up at Derek with interest. "You the groom?"

"Yes, ma'am," he replied, offering his hand. "Derek Cabot."

"You're a looker, Derek," she said, then stood on tiptoe and beckoned him to lean down. He complied and she added in a loud whisper, "But you got to work at this a little harder if she's forgetting that she wears your name."

A ripple of laughter passed among the women, except for Elizabeth who was still trying to recover from Babs's backhand. Edward and Caleb grinned at each other. Charlotte felt the color rise to her hairline.

Derek took the advice with a respectful nod. "You're absolutely right. I'll apply myself."

"Course, I understand Elizabeth and Kendra here stole you right out from your honeymoon to help save this shindig. No wonder the little lady's not sure of herself." She turned her full attention on Charlotte. "You're the one responsible for that dress Kendra's going to wear?"

The question had a suggestion of condemnation. Charlotte angled her chin because the dress was perfect for Kendra. "Yes, I am," she replied.

Babs nodded, treating her to the same backhand she'd given Elizabeth, except that this one landed on her elbow—and broke it, Charlotte was sure.

"Beautiful dress. Gives some class to this show. Only real thing here—except for my cake. Come on, I'll show you."

Babs locked Charlotte's wrist in one hand and Derek's in the other and headed off at a quick pace toward the back of the house.

Charlotte shrugged helplessly at the Farnsworths and their guests. "Excuse us," she said as she was tugged along.

Derek caught her eye over the much smaller woman's head and she could see that he was enjoying this. She had to admit she was, too. Babs was a delightful surprise in this stronghold of social correctness.

Derek was surprising also. Gone was the demanding, exacting man she'd so despised at the Farnsworth–Morreaux office. In his place was a casual, taunting, sexually aggressive man who was determined to find a chink in her armor before this week was over.

The laughter in his eyes drew her and charmed her. But she had to resist. She was here on business, though everyone else thought she was honeymooning in her spare time. And she wasn't about to let Derek Cabot seduce her just to prove to himself that he could.

The functional white kitchen was almost as big as a restaurant's and boasted every sophisticated aid and appliance that might be found in one. Charlotte had seen it before. The Farnsworth dinners were legendary.

A plump older woman in a serviceable apron looked up from arranging orange slices on salads. She smiled fondly at Babs, then recognized Charlotte.

"Congratulations on your wedding, Miss Morreaux," she said, turning an interested gaze on Derek. "Good morning, sir."

"Pauline, this is my husband, Derek Cabot," Charlotte said, horrified at how easily the words tripped off her tongue. "Derek, this is one of the finest cooks in all of southern California, Pauline Miller."

Unable to free himself from Babs's grip, Derek waved his free hand at her. "Nice to meet you, Pauline. I've enjoyed many of your dinners, though we've never met. I'm looking forward to lunch."

Pauline studied him a moment, then nodded at Charlotte. "Good work, Mrs. Cabot."

Babs freed her captives, then whipped the towel aside that covered a large pottery bowl of some deep vanilla-colored doughlike substance filled with nuts, raisins and other dried fruit.

"Smell that," she ordered the pair.

Simultaneously Charlotte and Derek obeyed, dipping faces several respectful inches from the substance.

Charlotte caught the tang of sourdough.

"Making it from my own starter," Babs said.

Though Charlotte wasn't much of a cook, she knew that a cup of starter was used to create new recipes, while flour and sugar and milk were added to the starter on a regular basis to keep it alive and growing.

It was a staple that had come west on wagon trains, moved to new homes with married daughters, was shared with neighbors and traveled along generations with a steadiness that was comforting to think about.

Derek leaned down to take a whiff and smelled the sweet, yeasty aroma of a living thing. Wrapped in the aroma was a floral fragrance that was Charlotte.

Charlotte felt his chin touch her hair, smelled the open-air fragrance of his after-shave and the light touch of his hand at her back as he leaned over her.

Everything inside her seemed to move just a little faster—heartbeat, breath, blood. She straightened abruptly.

Derek dodged her quick move and returned her suspicious look with one of innocence.

"I wanted to make Kennie's wedding cake with this," Babs said, lovingly replacing the cloth. "Brought the starter with me all the way from the Bitterroot Valley in Montana. But Lizzie says her guests won't understand if they don't have some mile-high thing from the spiffy bakery on Rodeo Drive.'' She rolled her eyes. "Going to have crystal birds on it." Then she sighed, smoothing the cloth with a gesture that was both thoughtful and sad. "So we're going to have this with dinner. Funny, isn't it, that all the homey old things don't fit in the world today. It's gotten so narrow and...and plain." She whispered, "That's why I never come here 'less I have to."

Charlotte put an arm around her and squeezed comfortingly. "I can't wait to taste it. Of course, I'm into old things, too, so I think it would be appropriate anywhere."

Babs smiled up at her, the sadness gone. It was apparent she'd long ago accepted that she and her daughter had little more than a blood connection.

"It's too bad I wasn't around to make a cake for *your* wedding."

Charlotte decided then and there to call her if the event ever came to be. "Well, it was kind of a quick thing. We didn't even have a cake."

Babs suddenly looked pleased about that. "Well, I'm going to make one, just for the two of you to share. You know, all the nuts and fruit in here promise fertility." She winked and waggled an arthritic index finger at Charlotte. "And with you forgetting your married name, it's bound to help."

Derek met her helpless glance and laughed softly.

"Thank you, Babs. I appreciate having you on my side."

"Mother? Mother!" Elizabeth's sharp voice sounded from the doorway. "I'd like Pauline to serve lunch now. Will you bring *the Cabots* out, please." There was a subtle emphasis on "the Cabots" that underlined her lack of conviction that that was indeed what they were.

"All right, all right." Babs pushed Charlotte and Derek before her with a roll of her eyes in Pauline's direction. "Let's go before Princess Grace has a hissy fit. I'll be back to help you serve, Pauline."

"Mrs. McGuffy, you're supposed to be a guest here," Pauline said, shooing her away. "I'll take care of things."

Babs dismissed her protests with a wave of her hand and led Charlotte and Derek toward the dining room. "Only society folk would decide cooking was too much work and hire someone to do it for them, then force that person to do it all by herself. Does that make sense to you?"

BABS BUSTLED in and out of the dining room, helping Pauline serve and clear away. Everyone accepted her sharp observations in stride, except Elizabeth who seemed torn between wanting to kill her mother and wanting to die herself.

Charlotte couldn't help enjoying her discomfort because it was all of her own making. Babs offended no one but Elizabeth and her inflated opinion of herself.

After lunch, Charlotte went upstairs to Kendra's room to look over the bridesmaids' dresses while the men closed themselves in Caleb's study. Elizabeth followed her mother into the kitchen, presumably to set down a few rules.

Charlotte had to admit that the dress from which she'd rescued Kendra was a beaded monstrosity. A high neck with padded shoulders was covered with sequins and bugle beads across the shoulders and tapered to a V at the waistline. Beading came up from the waist in a high, scalloped pattern.

It might have suited a taller, broader-shouldered woman—like Elizabeth—but it made Kendra look as though she'd donned a very expensive dress destined for the football field.

Sitting on the edge of Kendra's bed, Charlotte winced as Kendra did a turn in front of her.

"I can't believe that *this* is what came of mother's design! It cost her a fortune, and it's so ugly! She and Jean Michel are squabbling over whose fault it is."

Charlotte doubted there was any question. Elizabeth had probably had her mind set on what *she* wanted, forced the idea down Kendra's throat, then steamrolled Jean Michel into doing it.

Kendra pushed it over her head with little regard for the expensive beading and tossed it on the bed behind Charlotte. Then she slipped the beautiful Victorian dress over her head. It settled into place like a cloud, making Kendra beautiful despite her tumbled hair.

Briane, the redhead from Houston, came out of the bathroom with the broad-shouldered, full-skirted plum-colored dress Elizabeth had probably thought would carry on the theme of her creation.

Kendra and Briane looked at each other, frowning at the now discordant note of the soft, Victorian bridal dress, and the beautiful but blatantly contemporary bridesmaid gown.

Denise, the brunette, emerged from the next room in the same creation in purple. It looked even worse.

"What'll we do?" Kendra demanded plaintively.

Charlotte's love of the challenge fabrics and fashion took over and any resentment she might have felt for Kendra faded away. She could fix this little nightmare. What was more, she wanted to.

"Okay." She stood and studied the dresses with a critical eye. The dresses had a basic simple line that would be easy to turn into their purposes.

"Scissors," she said to Kendra.

"Scissors?" Kendra repeated worriedly.

"To remove the shoulder pads."

"Right." Kendra delved into a little desk across the room and returned with a pair of ornate embroidery scissors.

Charlotte reached into the shoulder of Briane's dress and began to snip.

"Watch it in there," Briane joked, careful not to move. "That's only a triple A, but it's precious to me."

Charlotte appreciated the woman's sense of humor. "Maybe we should stuff the shoulder pad down the bodice," she suggested.

Denise laughed. "With her luck, they'll slip and she'll walk down the aisle with a flat chest and well-developed kneecaps."

Everyone laughed at the absurd mental image.

"Okay." The pads removed, Charlotte smoothed the now pliant fabric over Briane's shoulder, stepped back and saw instant improvement.

"That's better, but it's so plain," Kendra said, grumbling.

"I was thinking…" Charlotte did a turn around the girls, who stood dutifully in place like a pair of mannequins. "I'll tailor the dropped shoulder, find tulle to match…" As she spoke she lifted the first layer of silky overskirt to bring it around Briane's shoulder. "And we'll make a small cape that we'll catch here with a little silk flower." She gathered the fabric at Briane's bosom, then looked up at Kendra for approval. "It'll be quick and easy to do, and it'll make the difference. What do you think?"

Kendra tilted her head right, then left, and smiled in disbelief. "I think it's perfect. But what about the headpieces?"

She took one of the little whimsies of netting lined up on the dresser and put the plum-colored one on Briane's head. It looked too contemporary for the dress's new look.

"It doesn't fit anymore, does it?"

"Picture hats would be nice," Denise said.

"But there isn't time to find them in the right colors," Kendra said worriedly. "Is there?"

Charlotte shook her head. "I don't think so. But we could make coronets of silk flowers or fresh flowers. That would be very Victorian."

"Fresh flowers would mean you'd have to do them at the last minute," Kendra said thoughtfully. "And what if something went wrong?"

Charlotte was beginning to think there was hope for Kendra. Elizabeth would never have considered that. She'd have thought fresh flowers the right choice and wouldn't have cared that someone would have to create them under great pressure at the last moment.

"I know where to go for silk flowers," Charlotte said. "And at the shop I have some dried flowers I could use and some pearls and beads that would add interest and make them unique."

The women nodded unanimously.

Kendra rummaged in a desk drawer and produced a small white envelope she handed to Charlotte. "Here are the swatches we used to have our shoes dyed, and I'll write you a check."

"Oh, don't," Charlotte said, following her when she went back to the desk. "I'll just get what we need and we'll settle up when we're sure everything . . . works."

Charlotte's attention was caught by a beautiful painting over Kendra's desk of a brass pot of flowers. The light in the brass gleamed warmth, and the softness of the flowers was almost touchable. She noticed the scripted *K* with which Kendra signed her sketches as a child.

"Kendra," she said in amazement. "I didn't know you were painting."

"I'm not, really." Kendra stepped back to give her painting a critical study. "I've taken a few classes when

Mother hasn't had me completely tied up in one of her guilds or leagues or clubs.''

"This should be hanging downstairs."

"Don't be silly." Kendra's tone was wry. "It didn't cost enough." Then, realizing she'd been critical of her mother's scale for success, she tossed her head and laughed lightly. "My style isn't unique enough to be noticed."

"Wouldn't devoting some time to it help you find your special . . . something?"

Kendra shrugged. "Maybe. But I have other plans now. I'm getting married."

"Kendra . . ." A thousand arguments rose to Charlotte's lips, but Briane came to lean a companionable elbow on Kendra's shoulder. "Are you lucky to have a friend who's a wedding expert!"

"Really." Denise hooked a thumb in the direction of the pile of beads on the bed. "You should have consulted her before you ordered this horrid dress."

Kendra looked at Charlotte, and for a moment there was more in her eyes than the spoiled young woman with whom she'd grown up. Though publicly she still seemed to be a clone of Elizabeth, something within her had changed.

A new connection was made between them. It had more to do with respect than affection, but it was there all the same.

"Thank you," Kendra said. "I appreciate your disrupting your honeymoon to do this for me."

Charlotte shrugged and slipped into her role. "You know how the men of Farnsworth–Morreaux are. Time away from the office is unheard of. Derek would rather be here than on some sunny beach.''

"I'm not going to let Trey be like that," Kendra said with quiet firmness.

Charlotte nodded. "More power to you. If you'll excuse me, I'll go hunt down what we need and let you know how it's going at dinner."

"Good. See you then."

Charlotte raced down the mahogany stairway, anxious to get as far away as possible from this movie set of a home and into the crowded, smog-shrouded, gaschoked reality of downtown Los Angeles.

She was all the way to the garages before she remembered that she didn't have a car. Then she turned in the direction of Derek's Porsche and wondered whether or not he had the keys on him.

The chauffeur, white sleeves rolled up, appeared from out of the shadows of the garage, a chamois in his hand. She knew him well. He'd driven her and Kendra many times when they'd been girls.

"Can I help you, Miss Morreaux? I mean, Mrs. Cabot?"

"Do you have Mr. Cabot's keys, Henry?" she asked.

"Yes, I do."

"May I have them, please?"

"Certainly." He disappeared into the shadows and returned again with a small brass ring of four or five keys.

He held it out to her and she was about to slip her index finger into the ring and take it from him when another male voice said with quiet command, "Don't even think about it."

Charlotte turned in guilty surprise to find Derek standing behind her.

"Oh..." she said with exaggerated brightness, then added for Henry's sake, "Darling. I thought you were in a meeting."

"I was." He replied, taking the keys from her hand. "I'm out. Going somewhere?"

"I, ah, have to pick up a few things for the brides-maids' dresses. Since my car is still in the shop, I was sure you wouldn't mind my taking yours." She smiled at Henry to remind Derek that he was there, and that he probably wouldn't understand any references to theft.

Derek gave Henry an even look. "Ever let your wife drive your cherry Mustang, Henry?"

Henry replied gravely. "Never, Mr. Cabot."

"Sound policy. I don't let Mrs. Cabot drive this." He grinned. "Remember that next time she asks you for my keys."

Henry nodded. "Right, sir."

Charlotte rolled her eyes. "I have never had an accident," she pointed out, looking at one man, then the other. "Can either of you say that?"

"I had an accident once," Henry admitted, "trying to get out of the way of a woman making a U-turn on a freeway on ramp."

Derek added, "And I was once rear ended by a woman trying to parallel park."

Charlotte put a hand over her eyes. "Well, I'd love to stand and listen to you two praise each other, but I have to get to Flowers and Fabrics in downtown Los Angeles. Would either of you two care to drive me?"

"My pleasure, ma'am," Henry said. "That's what Mrs. Farnsworth pays me for."

"Thanks, Henry," Derek said, giving his keys a toss. "I'll do it. You stay and protect the stable from other marauding women."

Henry laughed heartily. "If I'm approached by marauding women, they can have everything I've got."

Derek opened the passenger side door for Charlotte and grinned over her head at the chauffeur. "You're a man after my own heart, Henry Phillips."

"You know," Charlotte said as they backed out of the garage and turned in a tight circle to head down the driveway, "I am so grateful you're not my husband, I can't tell you."

He gave her a lazy smile. "I know you are. But before this is over, you'll wish I were. *You* might even propose to *me.*"

"In your dreams, Cabot."

"You are, Charlie," he said, shifting and sending the little car down the lane like a rocket. "You are."

Chapter Four

It was alarming, Charlotte thought, to be moving at top speed in the midst of six lanes of freeway traffic and look out the window into the face of a tire named General. Most cars looked enormous beside the small Porsche. Pickups looked huge, and semis freighting goods to and from the shipping capital of western America looked like Goliaths. One wrong move on Derek's part and they'd have been nothing more than a speck in the tread of some triple trailer.

"Nervous?" he asked, glancing her way as the traffic slowed at a popular off ramp.

"A little," she admitted, embarrassed to find she had sunken down in her already low seat.

"Is it me or the traffic?"

"You sit up a lot higher in the Duesenberg," she said, trying not to wince as the traffic moved on and he battled a van for a spot in the next lane and won. "I'm not used to watching the traffic from the viewpoint of the muffler. Haven't you ever thought about getting something bigger? Something higher?"

"This is more maneuverable. And I have good reflexes. You're safe, I promise you. This our exit?"

"Ah, yes. Then take a left. The shop's about three blocks down on the right side."

"Got it."

They were there in five minutes, and pulled effortlessly into an on-street spot that would have taken her ten minutes of inching forward and back with the Duesenberg. There might be advantages to this little car, she thought, but they were apparent only when one left the freeway.

Derek tossed his jacket in the back seat, then came around to help her out. The curb was higher than the floor of the car.

She bounced up beside him, ruffled and conscious of controlling her short, silky skirt.

"Geez!" she exclaimed, tugging everything back into place. "Climbing out of that thing is like rising out of a basement. Do I look like I've been working on a furnace or something?"

He grinned, reaching out intrepidly to refasten the pearly button that had come undone at her scooped neckline. "No, but my temperature's up," he said with a direct look into her eyes.

She looked back, determined not to blush. "There's no one watching now, Cabot. You can be yourself."

"This is it," he said.

"Derek..."

"One more thing."

"What?"

He took the angled-cut end of the black ribbon that secured her hair and tugged until the straight, blond mass fell free. He tossed the ribbon into the car and closed the door. "There." He studied her a moment, then reached a hand into the thick mass and combed his fingers downward through it. Something happened in his eyes—an emotion, a feeling, appeared there she couldn't analyze.

"It feels," he said seriously, "like the music from a cello."

She stared up at him, snared by the velvet darkness of his eyes. And by the thought. Her mind played back a melody she'd once heard in a cello solo; she didn't remember where or when. It had been smooth and honeyed and heartbreaking.

He put an arm around her and led her into the shop.

RELAX, DEREK TOLD himself as he trailed after Charlotte while she wandered from aisle to aisle. The store was acres of fabric in every shade of every color and every texture the mind could conceive. You know yourself. You do chancy things all the time. It's a large part of your success.

But this is a woman, he argued with himself, not a business deal. A fearless, aggressive approach was more likely to frighten than stun or impress. What's called for here is a little style, man. Rein in the horses. And keep your hands in your pockets.

She stopped so abruptly he collided with her. She gave him a quick, apologetic smile over her shoulder, obviously only vaguely aware of him. The moment they walked into the store, she seemed to have turned into someone else.

She pulled a bolt of purple stuff off a table and tried to put it in his hands. "Would you hold this, please?"

He made a reluctant sound, looking around, afraid he might be recognized. "Do I have to?"

She looked first surprised, then exasperated. "Yes, you have to. I've been humiliated on more than one occasion, thanks to your quick thinking to save my stepmother. You can do this little thing for me."

He resisted when she tried to hand it to him again.

"You'll have to make it worth my while," he warned.

She studied him a full ten seconds before she asked in dry tones, "And what would that entail?"

"Something wifely," he replied. "A back rub. A kiss for no reason."

She turned to place the bolt atop the other bolts to unroll it and check the shade, but the surface was already a jumble of bolts that hadn't been replaced. She turned back to him, exasperated. His hands would provide the only flat surface around.

"You have the duration of our stay at the guest house in which to do this," he encouraged.

She pushed the bolt at him, sure she would find a way to evade him.

The bolt bounced in his arms as she unrolled it, then he found himself looking at her through a haze of pale purple gossamer.

"Perfect," she said, rolling the fabric back up and plunking it back in his arms. She pulled out a bolt of a deeper, redder purple. Pleased with herself, she smiled at him and turned him toward a row of carts.

"Let's get something to put these in," she said, "before I have to bargain away my virtue."

"Two bolts," he said, holding them to him possessively when she tried to take them from him and drop them into a cart. "That means I get the rub *and* the kiss."

Charlotte shook her head at him, holding back a smile through sheer cussedness. "No wonder Daddy has you negotiate all contracts. Come on. I want to look at the silk flowers."

"Oh, God."

A second room at the back of the store held the silk representation of every species and subspecies of flower known to man, in their genuine colors and in some creative applications.

"A brown rose?" Derek plucked one from a trellis that attempted to make them appear real. "I've never seen a brown rose."

She replaced the rose, then tucked her hand in his elbow and pulled him from the display of full-blown roses to the smaller tea variety, and pushed him gently around the back of the floor-to-ceiling cascade. "I'm looking for a lavender rose—a delicate shade that'll coordinate with both of these." She held out the fabric swatches of plum and purple. "You try the back."

"Lavender roses?" he asked doubtfully, doing as she asked. "I've never seen that, either."

"Well, you obviously haven't sent many roses," she said, reaching for one that looked promising, then deciding it was too cool a color. "The Sterling Silver, a beautiful lavender rose, was developed years ago. And I think there've been others since then."

"When I send roses," he said, his voice sounding vaguely distracted as she lost sight of him around the wide display. "They're red."

"That's so conventional."

"It says something personal," he replied. "It doesn't say, 'I looked all over to find you an exclusive hybrid created in some laboratory because God didn't want it that color.' It says..."

She came face-to-face with him suddenly around the side of the display. She straightened with a start as he pinned her against the silky bank of roses, his eyes dark and challenging. "'These red roses express my passion for you, the color of my heart, my blood, my fire.'"

She looked back at him, her pulse tripping, her lips parted in surprise and the subtle beginnings of excitement. It occurred to her that excitement was a strange thing to find in a shop filled with fabric and silk flowers, but he seemed to create his own atmosphere, his own reality.

"I would never send you a lavender rose," he said, taking a step back and allowing her finally to draw an even breath.

He drew a dusky-rose flower from behind his back and held it out to her. "This it?"

"Ah, yes, I think so." She held the swatches to it and found that the strong but misty shade suited both. "Exactly right." She smiled up at him, hoping that confronting the attraction she felt would free the mystery inherent in it and make it disappear.

"You might be wasted in the corporate world, too," she said, following him around the display to the right shade. "Want to come to work for me?"

The roses were higher than she could reach, and she waited while he plucked down several dozen.

"Tempting as that is in some ways," he said, "I need the excitement of world-class deals and dangerous chances."

She studied him consideringly as he dropped the last rose in the cart. "Those don't sound like the preferences of a man who'd send red roses." She was gaining a new perspective on him. "I think you're more complex than you appear. Possibly even than you yourself realize."

He was beginning to suspect that himself. "What now?"

"Umm..." She looked around, her hand on the front of the cart. "Baby's breath, and those little five-petal purple things. And maybe some tiny beads."

"Lead on."

He watched her rummage through a deep bin of tiny flowers. With a silky rose in one hand, she brought flower after flower up to hold against it until she found the right shade.

"You know, speaking of complexity," he said, pulling up a flower and touching it to hers to check the shade, "you're an interesting case. What made a young woman who was left at the altar go into the wedding business? Isn't that a little masochistic?"

"No." She lifted a handful of flowers and uncovered a vein of little five-petal things in the right shade. Derek dutifully tossed them into the cart. "These other weddings have nothing to do with me," she said, replacing the top layer of flowers and smoothing them into place. "My business is to lend romance to the weddings with my dresses and my finishing touches. It's business. I'm removed from any personal involvement."

"Charlie," he scolded softly. "That's a crock."

In the middle of the aisle, with silk flowers of every color cascading all around them, she turned to him in mild annoyance. "And how do you know that?"

"I worked with you for a year. You become personally involved in everything you do. And I remember how you lit up when Prentiss walked into the room. You certainly can't claim to have no emotional involvement in this particular wedding."

She rolled her eyes and took control of the cart. "That doesn't mean that Borrowed Magic can't do its job."

"As I've pointed out before," he said, following her to a display of beads and beaded garlands at the far end of the shop. "You are Borrowed Magic. Maybe it would be healthier to admit that it's just a little painful."

"It isn't," she said, fingering the garlands festooning another trellis. She reached for one with beads no larger than the head of a pin. "I don't care anymore."

"About Trey or about getting married?"

"Both."

"Is that why you find it so difficult to pretend to be married to me?"

She unhooked the fine-beaded garland and looked for a moment as though she would like to strangle him with it.

"I find it difficult," she said, enunciating slowly, "because it's a deception that is going to trip us up and embarrass everyone."

"It won't," he said, "if you just relax and go with it." He studied her eyes for a moment, then asked with sudden insight, "Or is it too difficult to pretend that you really married someone?"

Charlotte closed her eyes and drew a deep breath. When she opened them again, he saw wariness in them, a little residual anger and a confusion she did not appear to want to deal with.

"You have two choices," she said, tightening her grip on the pearl garland. "Being garroted by a string of beads, or being quiet."

It was only when the words were out of her mouth and she was looking into his intrepid grin that she remembered his claim to love the challenge of world-class deals and dangerous chances.

She dropped her threatening pose. "You're not afraid of me," she said. "Is that what you're trying to tell me?"

He laughed, thinking how genuine she was under the Duchess of Winter cloak.

"Actually," he said, growing serious suddenly and cupping the back of her head in his hand, "on a level I don't really understand—I think I am."

She was stunned by his admission. So stunned, that when he lowered his head to kiss her, she couldn't step back.

His mouth was warm, gentle, coaxing. It held none of the bold assumption of control that had been intended to confuse Bitsy at the shower the previous afternoon.

This was a communication between them, tender and warm, an experience of touch, a probing of sensations, physical and emotional. It seemed to chip at a resistance that was already peeling away.

Derek had dreamed for months of holding her unresisting body in his arms. And now he had it—in the middle of a fabric store. Fate had the damnedest sense of humor.

When he felt her lean against him, he forgot where they were and thought only of who they were—man and woman. He felt the potential ripen between them as she responded with a closemouthed but heartfelt kiss.

He fought against the need to part her lips, and simply paid her back in kind. It wasn't nobility that drove him. It was the knowledge he'd learned while working with her that, once pushed, she tuned out and turned off. And that was precisely the reverse of what he wanted.

Charlotte needed more, but was afraid to initiate it. Pretending to be husband and wife, they were in a precarious position and she didn't want him to misunderstand. She didn't want him to think—she didn't want him to *know*—she was just beginning to understand the tension that had always existed between them.

If she opened her mouth under his, he would think she wanted to explore it and she didn't. She was smarter than that.

She pulled away and looked up at him, a little surprised he hadn't insisted on more. And just a little disappointed.

"We have to be back in time for dinner," she said faintly. "Babs talked Pauline into making stew."

He nodded, catching the corner of his bottom lip in strong white teeth as though the touch of hers might linger there. The notion pleased her.

"We'll have time to pursue this later."

She tried to pull herself out of the warm languor his embrace and his kiss had caused. She smoothed her dress and tossed her hair back. "I don't think that would be a good idea," she said briskly.

He dissolved her briskness first with that deadly smile, then with a quick but thorough kiss.

"With all due respect," he said, pausing to wink at a pair of high-school girls whose cart contained all kinds of things in purple and gold, "who listens to you?"

As the girls moved on, still staring at him over their shoulders with dreamy expressions, Charlotte reached up to the trellis for two more strings of tiny beads and seriously considered winding them around her own throat.

He *did* have a thing for danger, but he wasn't dragging her into it. He wasn't. She pushed the cart toward the checkout stand, leaving him to follow, and admitted to herself that her denial sounded very, very thin.

THOUGH THE GUESTS had been in residence only a day, Charlotte noticed that the happiness and charm inherent in a wedding were taking over the formal correctness Elizabeth always applied to everything.

Seated together at one corner of the table, Kendra, Briane and Denise laughed uproariously and continuously. Charlotte watched in fascination. This was a side of Kendra she'd never seen, a side that had apparently developed in Gstaad and Cozumel with her friends and become a part of her makeup—a part Elizabeth couldn't affect. Judging by Elizabeth's frowning concern, she had tried and failed.

Edward, Caleb and Derek were engrossed in business talk at the other end of the table, while Caroline bubbled over to a distracted Elizabeth about the beautiful array of gifts arriving daily that had been set out in the parlor.

Trey and Charlotte, seated across from each other, were forced to find something to talk about.

"Isn't this stew wonderful?" she asked, thinking as she heard her own words that as a conversational gambit it was pathetic. Still, it was *some*thing and she wouldn't let it go. She tapped the side of the small round of bread that had been hollowed out to accommodate the stew.

"Imagine serving it in a bread," she said. "I've never seen that before. I wonder why it doesn't leak out?"

Trey looked at her for a moment as though considering whether or not the question was important enough to answer. Then he said politely, "I imagine because the stew is thick, the bread inside soaks up the liquid, and the crusty outside seals it all in."

Very well thought out, very logical. She had once admired that he could be so intelligent as well as romantic. Had that been just a year ago? It seemed like an age.

"What are you doing in the company these days?" she asked. "I haven't kept up very well since I opened Borrowed Magic."

"Windsor Tech's administrative offices are in London," he replied, looking modestly pleased with himself. "When our deal goes through, Edward and Caleb are sending me there to restructure. I've always kind of felt like London was my city."

"Paris is mine," Charlotte said dreamily, forgetting the awkwardness between them. "I spent the most wonderful summer of my life in Paris when I was about twenty. Montparnasse, Notre Dame and the Place du Parvis, soup at Bistro Allard." She sighed. "I think it was Paris that made me fall in love with the old and the romantic."

Something subtle flickered in his eyes. She saw it and felt a vague sense of alarm, though she didn't know why.

"So you haven't changed?"

She looked around the table and noted that everyone was still engrossed in their conversations. She wasn't sure why she should feel uncomfortable answering that question, but she did.

"No," she replied. Then couldn't resist asking, "Have you?"

"Yes, I think so," he replied, glancing Kendra's way. She and Briane were leaning on each other in laughter. "I have a better understanding of what I need."

She smiled. "I'm happy for you." Then added to herself, *I wish I knew what I needed. I used to think I knew until you botched it up for me. Ah, well. Lucky escape.*

"And I'm happy for you," he said, indicating Derek with a jut of his chin. The look in his eye held a grudging respect coupled with an obvious dislike. "You got the man who never has to think twice about anything."

Charlotte turned to Derek, who had pushed his plate aside and listened while her father and Caleb talked about Windsor's London office. Though impeccably groomed in a pin-striped suit, dark hair combed slickly back, except for a loose wave at his precise side part, he did not look like social-register material.

He looked like what he said he was—a man with angles and edges made to deflect the danger he loved to challenge. Yet overlaying that was a veneer of charm that might deceive one into thinking otherwise, that worked in his favor when he made those world-class deals. She'd seen him in action. He seduced with that charm, then moved in for the kill with a wit and intelligence that had startled even the young woman who'd grown up in Edward Morreaux's household.

She put a hand on his arm, partly to prove possession to Trey, and partly because she felt a need to.

He turned at her touch, an eyebrow raised in question. Then he glanced at Trey and drew his own conclusion. He placed his other hand over hers and leaned forward to kiss her cheek.

"You'll have my undivided attention later," he said in a low voice rich with sexual suggestion, "I promise." Then he turned back to Edward and Caleb.

Had they been truly married, she'd have been annoyed at playing second fiddle to a business discussion. But as it was, the little ploy was effective in convincing Trey that Derek wanted her—a satisfaction she found it difficult to deny herself.

Charlotte turned back to the table to find that Elizabeth and Caroline had been watching also. Caroline looked delighted. Elizabeth's suspicions looked just a little shaken.

After dinner Trey and Kendra took Briane and Denise to a Karaoke bar.

"Oh, come with us," Briane coaxed Charlotte and Derek. "If Denise even *looks* as though she's going to get up and sing 'Memories,' I'll sedate her, I promise."

Charlotte refused with a smiling shake of her head.

Derek hooked an arm around Charlotte's neck and said, "Thanks, anyway. Neither of us can carry a tune in a bucket. And I think Charlie wanted to work on your dresses tonight."

"You found everything?" Kendra asked. "My goodness, I'd left it to you so completely, I forgot to worry about it."

Charlotte nodded. "If you don't mind, I'll take the dresses to the guest house where there's a little less distraction and work on them there. I should have one of the capes for someone to try on tomorrow morning. If it's all right, the other will be easy."

Denise looked at Charlotte with admiration. "When and if I get married, I'm sending for you to come to Boston." Then she added impishly, "You're sure you don't want to come and listen to me sing 'Memories'?"

Briane and Kendra turned on her simultaneously.

"I was kidding!" she insisted as the other two dragged her off toward the door. Trey followed in their wake, gathering his jacket and Kendra's, looking as though he could think of preferable ways to spend the evening than in a Karaoke bar with three rowdy women.

"You two get to bed early," Caroline encouraged with a straight face as Elizabeth handed Charlotte Briane's dress stored in a zippered plastic sleeve. "Don't let her work all night, Derek."

He smiled quietly back. "Never fear," he said with a quality in his tone that made Caroline beam and Edward look at his daughter and his right-hand man in sudden interest.

Charlotte hurried off down the walk.

"I *wish*," she growled at him when he caught up with her, "that you wouldn't do that." She waggled a fist under his nose. "One day you're going to say something in that suave, seductive voice and I'm going to let you have it!"

"Your fist?" he asked. "Or the seduction?"

She made a small sound of pain and continued to march toward the guest house. "The only thing that saved you," she grumbled, "is that Bitsy Tate wasn't there to write everything down."

"Where was she, anyway?"

"At the Karaoke bar, presumably setting up to record the happy couple humiliating themselves for posterity."

She stepped aside at the door of the guest house to let him unlock it. He frowned at her as he inserted the key. "You're serious?"

"Yes. It's the wedding of the decade. Nosy people want to know every lurid little detail. The Karaoke bar will make a great side story for the tabloids."

"She wouldn't do that as a guest in their home," Derek said. Then at Charlotte's look that proclaimed him a naive innocent, he added with a grin, "No kidding? Then we'd better watch our step. I'm not wild about ending up on the cover of the *Enquirer.*"

Charlotte raised a haughty eyebrow as he ushered her inside. "You're the one in danger," she said. "I've been humiliated to cinders once already. I'd hardly notice a second time." She mimicked a tough-girl voice. "So don't push me or I'll spill my guts to the press."

He caught her arm as she would have walked past him to the bedroom. He took the dress from her and tossed it onto the sofa, then looked down into her eyes. His own were darkened by the early-evening shadows. His hands were a painless but firm pressure on her upper arms.

"I want to warn you," he said quietly, "that it's dangerous to threaten me."

She believed him without question. But it was important that he believe she would do as she promised.

"And you should know," she countered, "that I'm still Edward Morreaux's little girl, and if he thought you'd done anything to hurt me, or frighten me, your career on this continent—on this planet—would be over in a heartbeat."

His grip on her tightened. "That was another threat."

"It was a warning," she said, trying not to wince, "that you're not the only one with power."

"At least I'm using my own."

That annoyed her because it was true. "No, you're not," she said angrily. "You're using the power you acquired by putting me in this combustible position. If we weren't caught in this stupid farce, I'd simply slap your face and go home."

"You know," he said, dropping his hands from her to fold his arms, "it's interesting that you think of me in such violent terms. At the office you were always threatening to knock my block off, or sock me in the kisser. Do you read Sam Spade before you go to bed, or are your feelings for me so strong and so suppressed that they erupt in images of hot physical action?"

"Oh, please. I wouldn't...!"

Charlotte's angry denial was quickly arrested when he caught a handful of her hair and brought her to him.

Fear and excitement rose simultaneously within her. "If you try to kiss me now," she warned, her head tilted back because of his grip on her hair, "you'll need a lip transplant. Trust me on this."

"Bitsy and her photographer are coming up the walk," Derek said sotto voce, leaning over her like Rhett over a helpless Scarlett. "And the door is open. Unless you were absolutely sincere about not noticing a second humiliation, you'd better follow my lead."

They stared at each other for an instant, two strong wills challenged, two cherished careers in danger of falling victim to Bitsy's Tidbits.

Resigned to her fate, Charlotte was aware of his large hand completely cupping her head, of the scent of roses that wafted in from the garden, of Bitsy's gasp as she and Darby walked along the path—and stopped.

Derek lowered his head and, caught between fury and fire, Charlotte parted her lips.

Chapter Five

Derek congratulated himself on maximum use of a slim advantage. Edward always said it was his best strength.

Personally he didn't give a damn what Bitsy Tate thought or wrote, but it was becoming a good tool with which to assure himself of Charlotte's cooperation.

And her cooperation delighted him. He felt her slim arms come around his neck, then a hand wandered over his ear and into his hair.

Sensation raced over his scalp and down his spine. When she touched the inside of his mouth with the tip of her tongue, he forgot who was watching and why.

His tongue parried and teased, turned her hesitant foray into his mouth into a battle for supremacy.

Her heart racing, her body flushed, she returned kiss for kiss, nibble for nibble, drinking from his mouth as he drank from hers. She finally lost the battle when she had to draw away to gulp in air. It was a loud sound in the quiet, darkening evening.

Then it was followed by a little cry of surprise when Derek lifted her off her feet, kissed her long and reverently and turned to the bedroom.

Over his shoulder, her eyelids heavy with passion, Charlotte saw Bitsy staring openmouthed, Darby looking wistful.

The bedroom was cool, the corners filled with shadows as Derek kicked the door closed, then leaned against it. He expelled a long groan of a sigh, then walked forward several paces to drop Charlotte in the middle of the bed.

For one instant of ambivalence, she wondered if he might join her. But he went to the small walnut chair at the foot of the bed and sank into it like a man who couldn't stand up another moment.

"Either you've had a private craving for my body from the moment we met," he said, stretching his legs out and letting his arms fall over the sides of the chair. "Or you're the next Meryl Streep."

Charlotte remained supine on the cool bedspread, unwilling to sit up and look into his eyes.

"Well . . ." she said softly, "there's a lot at stake."

"I thought you said you wouldn't mind being humiliated a second time."

It was easier to admit she'd lied about that than that she *had* always wondered what he'd be like as a lover, and that the need for an answer grew more demanding every time he touched her.

"So I exaggerated. I'd rather Bitsy thinks I'm this saintly woman who'll come to the rescue of her ex-fiancé's current fiancée. It's worth more to me to walk away from this with my dignity and my good business name intact than to expose you for the villain that you are."

"Expose me," he repeated thoughtfully. "Interesting choice of words. You have been repressing, haven't you?"

"Don't you have something to do," she asked lightly, "that would involve leaving the room?"

"No," he replied lazily. Then he straightened and pushed himself to his feet. "But I guess I should if you're going to get to work on that dress."

He went to the light switch to flip it on.

"Don't do that!" Charlotte said urgently.

He stopped, his hand suspended. "Why not?"

"If Bitsy's watching the house, which I wouldn't put past her, she'll wonder why we put a light on when you carried me in here obviously intent on . . . you know."

Derek flipped the switch, filling the room with intrusive, artificial light. Charlotte sat up indignantly.

"Relax," he said, coming to the bed and smoothing the tumbled hair from her face with a warm, gentle hand. "She'll think I put the light on so that I can look at you."

She stared up at him, unable to form one coherent word.

"And she'd be right," he added softly, giving her chin a playful pinch. Then he turned to the door. "I'll bring you the dress and put on the coffee."

"How DOES it look?"

Derek, stretched out on the sofa with the latest escapade of Spenser, Robert B. Parker's fictional private detective, looked up to focus on Charlotte. It was after midnight.

She had fashioned a narrow, gauzy cape for the plum-colored dress, and had fastened it at the little dip just above the delicate swell of her breasts with a little bunch of the five-petaled purple flowers. Under it, she wore the dress Briane would wear the day of the wedding.

She had twisted her blond hair up and out of the way, and he felt himself go weak at the perfect line of her long, slender neck and softly sloped shoulder. The need to put his lips there was like a primal force. He had to give himself a minute to find his voice.

"The cape looks lovely," he replied gravely. "You look indescribably beautiful."

She fluffed out the skirt a little nervously. "It is a beautiful dress. I was trying to give it a demure Victorian look. Does it work?"

He cleared his throat. "Well, I might not be the best one to ask. I find it more alluring than demure, but then I'm the type who always looks under and around things to see what's there."

She had to laugh. "I imagine that's gotten you into trouble on more than one occasion."

"It has," he admitted candidly, "but the satisfaction of knowing was always worth it. Turn around."

She complied, this time showing him the beautiful shape of her well-formed back, and the intriguing column of her neck against which wisps of hair lay in tempting disarray.

He had to think about something else.

"What are you going to do with all the flowers we bought this afternoon? And the beads?"

"Garlands for their hair," she replied, her eyes sparking with enthusiasm. "I'll be working on those as soon as I have the capes finished."

He smiled, sharing her obvious delight. "You really do love this stuff, don't you?"

She shrugged a beautiful, gauze-covered shoulder. "It's me. The slow, laid-back romantic you so despised in the office."

He put the book aside and stood. "For the last time," he said, "I didn't despise you. Anyway, you should be grateful to me. If it wasn't for the fact that *you* despised *me,* you'd still be at Farnsworth–Morreaux instead of doing what you love to do."

She looked at him for a long moment, long enough that he raised an eyebrow in question. She opened her mouth to say something, then changed her mind and turned to the bedroom.

"What?" he asked, hoping for a translation of that curious expression.

She turned at the bedroom door, studied him a moment, then relaxed against the molding as though reaching a decision that removed some burden from her.

"I didn't despise you, either," she admitted. "In fact, when you weren't shouting at me, I thought you were pretty interesting."

That was hard to let pass. He took several steady steps forward, but knew when to stop. He asked from several feet away from her, "You want to know just how interesting?"

She met his eyes and he saw the answer. His heart thumped against his ribs.

"I do," she replied finally, softly, "but I want to know a few other things first."

What? he wanted to say. Ask me anything. But she had smiled enigmatically and closed the door.

He went into the kitchen to make a fresh pot of coffee. It wouldn't prevent him from sleeping—Charlotte had already accomplished that.

CHARLOTTE SMELLED Derek's toothpaste and aftershave before she even opened her eyes. Anger rose hotly in her at the realization that he lay beside her. On the heels of their mellow mood of the night before, his assumption of sexual privileges made her furious. But she was determined not to give him the satisfaction of a display of temper.

"What are you doing in the bed?" she asked coolly without opening her eyes.

"Bitsy," he replied calmly, "is in the garden behind us with binoculars."

She opened her eyes at that and rolled her head on the pillow to look into his eyes. "You're kidding!" she whispered.

He lay beside her, his hips covered in a towel, his hands crossed over his stomach. "I'm not. I brought you a cup of coffee to help you wake up and saw her through the window. Do you leave your drapes open at home when you go to bed?" The question held disapproval.

"No," she replied. "But I don't have roses outside my bedroom window, either. So what do we do now?"

He smiled at the ceiling. "I could take off my towel."

"Choice number two, please," she said.

"Ah, Charlie," he said plaintively, "what is romance without imagination? Choice number two is that you kiss me good-morning, I pass you your cup of coffee, and we snuggle up to discuss the day."

"Derek," she said, "you're taking shameless advantage of the situation."

He stared at her a moment, apparently confused that she should be surprised. "Of course."

He was leaning over her, his bright dark eyes a threat to her sense of self-preservation. But the aroma of freshly brewed coffee wafted past his shoulder and under her nose.

"The coffee does smell wonderful," she said, waffling.

He gave her a knowing smile. "You can tell yourself it's really the coffee you want if that makes you feel better."

She raised an imperious eyebrow. "It is the coffee I want."

"Sure. Then give me what I want."

To confound Bitsy, and to wipe that self-satisfied look off Derek's face, Charlotte applied herself to the work of deception.

She put a small, but strong hand to Derek's bare shoulder and pushed him back against the pillow. She tried not to dwell on the warm, suedelike texture of the flesh under her fingertips, of the muscled chest she felt against the thin fabric of her nightgown as she leaned over him.

She saw surprise register in his eyes, then lazy pleasure as he lay back, apparently willing to let her assume control.

She gave the kiss everything she had—and she was a little alarmed to find that she had so much. Desire burst from her the moment she covered his mouth with hers. Memories of the other kisses they'd shared rose up in her memory to make her eager to share this one. That, combined with the need to show him she could wield a little power, too, made her aggressive but artful.

Derek was sure he was in heaven. When she knelt astride him and covered his face with kisses, he thought he might be hallucinating. When the kisses trailed down between his pecs and over the jut of his ribs, he knew he'd died and gone to heaven. When the kisses stopped at the barrier of his towel, he thought he'd caught a glimpse of what hell could be like.

"Don't stop," he said, his voice hoarse, "she might still be watching."

Charlotte sat back on her heels, a Duchess of Winter tilt to her chin and the downward cast of her eyes.

"She just walked away."

It surprised him a little that he hadn't seen that move coming on her part. After all, it was a page out of his own book. Take a small advantage and make the best of it. It did surprise him to find that he wasn't annoyed. He was now more intrigued than ever, and more determined to uncover—hopefully literally one day— the woman under the duchess.

He laced his hands behind his head and grinned up at her. "You must have really wanted that coffee."

She reached across him for the cup and saucer. He resisted the impulse to sample the thinly covered delicacies that moved forward, then back, within an inch of his lips.

"Deception is the key, isn't it?" she asked, backing carefully on her knees off the bed.

"It is," he called after her as she headed for the bathroom, his eye on the tempting sway of creamy flesh under the flimsy little gown, "as long as you don't deceive yourself!"

"YOU'RE A GENIUS," Kendra said in amazement, looking over Briane's shoulder into the cheval mirror.

The cape fell delicately from Briane's shoulders, the precise shade of the dress, the very touch the garment needed to take it from the modern gown it had been, to the more old-fashioned but demure dress it had become.

Denise looked over Kendra's shoulder with a smile of amazement. "How can that little bit of fabric make so much difference? I can't believe how right it looks."

Briane lifted one side of the flimsy little cape and smiled at her reflection. "I deserve to look wonderful, since I *didn't* get to sing 'Memories,' after all."

"Oh!" Her friends turned on her instantly, playfully swatting and teasing. Charlotte took the other dress and returned to the guest house to work on the cape.

Derek, Trey, Edward and Caleb were closeted in Caleb's den, and she planned to enjoy the quiet that had been such a part of her life before she'd answered Kendra's call for help and attended the shower.

Sunshine poured through the window of the little bedroom where she'd set up her portable sewing machine on an end table and pulled up the bedroom chair. Through the open window, she heard the birds singing happily, and inhaled the fragrance of the rose garden.

With such aesthetic accompaniments, the work should have been easy. Unfortunately the open window and the roses reminded her of that morning and made it difficult to roll a straight hem on Denise's plum-colored cape.

The worst part was that the memories were not unpleasant. They were delicious. They reminded her of how much she'd missed since she'd decided to bow out of man-woman relationships. More than that—they made her realize how much she had yet to experience. Derek had made her feel things, want things, she used to think were fantasies. Maybe they were, but now they were hers.

She worked through lunch and was just beginning to feel as though she were making headway when a rap on the door brought her head up.

"Yes?" she called.

There was an instant's silence, then a male voice called back quietly, "It's Trey."

For an instant, Charlotte stared at the door. Something told her letting him in would not be a wise move, but she put it down to unnecessary discomfort over the situation and thought it important that he not know she felt any.

She opened the door wide and gave him her warmest smile. "Hi," she said cheerfully. "Kendra isn't here. I think the girls said something about going to Rodeo Drive for a few last-minute things she needed for her trousseau."

He nodded, his hands in the pockets of raw-linen pants. A soft yellow sweater covered his long, lean torso. His rangy, athletic form once used to make her heart beat faster. She stood still for an instant, waiting for it to happen. Nothing.

"I know," he said. He gave her a charmingly embarrassed under-the-eyebrows look. "I wasn't looking for Kendra—I was looking for you."

"Really?" She tried to sound only mildly interested.

"I need to talk to you," he said, glancing over his shoulder as though concerned about being discovered. "Preferably while Bitsy is going over the reception menu with Elizabeth."

Dodging Bitsy seemed to be becoming a major part of everyone's life.

"What did you want to talk about?"

"Can we talk inside?"

"Trey..." she began, prepared to refuse him entry.

"Charlie, please," he said quietly, "there are some things I need to get off my chest."

An apology was the last thing she wanted to hear, but she didn't think she could in all conscience deny him the basic right to explain himself.

She stepped aside and gestured him into the small living room. He took the chair that faced the sofa, and she went into the kitchen for the coffeepot and two cups. After pouring, she settled in the corner of the sofa farthest away from him.

Trey left his cup on the table and leaned forward in his chair, bracing his elbows on his knees. His gray eyes were apologetic.

"First, I want to thank you for helping Kendra when it must be awkward for you. She told me at lunch how you've fixed the bridesmaids' dresses to coordinate with the dress you brought for her."

A sweep of her hand dismissed it as a problem. "Her father and mine have been friends for a long time."

"But you're still honeymooning," he said. "I don't suppose that occurred to her. She is spoiled."

His disloyalty to Kendra annoyed her. "So I've been told about myself on more than one occasion."

"No," he said. "You've been indulged, but you haven't been spoiled. There's a difference. In fact, I think it's a little shameful of Kendra and her mother to have called for your help on this, considering that you and I were once involved. They had to know it would be hard for you."

She shook her head serenely and lied through her teeth. "It hasn't been. Briane and Denise are fun to work with, and I've really enjoyed meeting Babs."

He straightened and sighed. "So you really don't care at all anymore?"

Thin ice, she warned herself, but found there were a few things she had to get off her own chest.

"Trey, you left me standing at the church in front of four hundred people. That tends to change a woman's feelings for a man."

He seemed almost pleased by that flash of temper. Then he hung his head. "I know, I know. I was a rat, a clod, an idiot, a louse..."

He looked up at her, and she said calmly, "You may continue."

He leaned against the back of the chair and raised his eyes to the ceiling. "What can I say? There isn't a word bad enough to describe what I did to you, and none strong enough to tell you how often and how much I've regretted it."

"Thank you," she said. "I appreciate knowing it gave you a few bad moments, too. But now it's over and the best thing you can do for all of us is not give it another thought."

"How can I do that?"

"By concentrating on your fiancée."

He sighed again. "My fiancée is concentrating on her friends. I've hardly been alone with her since they arrived."

"Then think about your promotion and your office in London," she said a little airily. "A woman tends to be a little distracted by the details of her wedding, particularly when her mother is determined to make it the cover story for *Bride* magazine. And it's been a while since she's seen her friends. They're such a relief from the company she and her mother usually keep. Give her a break."

He caught her gaze across the width of the coffee table. "You, on the other hand, were always doing thoughtful little things for me. You never forgot I was around. I didn't realize then how precious a commodity is a woman's complete attention."

Twit, she thought. Aloud, she said generously, "That's life. Live and learn. We often don't realize what we have until we've lost it."

He stood and paced across the room. "In defense of myself," he said in quiet but what seemed genuine dismay, "I can explain my behavior only by saying that I realized you were more than I could handle."

"What you *didn't* realize," she said, "was that you wouldn't have *had* to handle me. I'm able to handle myself. You'd have had only to love me."

"I know that now," he said with a regretful glance down at her that touched her as nothing he'd said previously had. "At the time, I felt threatened and overwhelmed."

She felt his sadness and her own, but under it all was the knowledge that it was over, and that she'd moved beyond the woman she'd been when she'd loved Trey. She tried not to bemoan the fact that he had someone and she didn't.

"I think you and Kendra will be very happy," she said, getting to her feet and ushering him to the door. "Things have a way of working out."

She pulled the door open. He walked reluctantly through and said with that sadness still in his eyes, "But she isn't you. Ooof!"

Trey had turned to make a dramatic exit and collided with Derek coming up the steps.

"Sorry," Trey said with a quick, guilty look at him. Then he moved around him and hurried down the walk back to the big house.

Derek stepped inside and pushed the door closed behind him. The flicker of jealousy he'd felt when he'd been coming up the walk and saw Trey standing in the open doorway ignited inside him like a tree struck by lightning.

He tossed his briefcase on the chair and confronted Charlotte, hands on his hips.

"Why don't you just invite Bitsy in for tea and tell her this is all a scripted performance?"

Surprised by his vehemence, Charlotte folded her arms and faced him down. She knew she looked guilty. She *felt* guilty, but she she also knew guilt was simply the by-product of the circumstances.

"We were just talking," she said calmly, "and Bitsy is in the kitchen with Elizabeth and Pauline, going over the menu for the reception."

"Bitsy," he said significantly, "was right behind me when I left the house."

She refused to betray concern. "So? She's a reporter. Hopefully she'll be less likely to jump to conclusions than you are."

He gave her the same pitying look she'd once given him when he'd suggested the same to her. "Please," he said dryly. "What did he want?"

"To talk to me."

"About what?"

That did it. He continued to stand there, feet planted like an inquisitor, fully expecting her to relate in detail the few moments she'd spent with Trey.

"This is a charade, remember!" she shouted at him. She wasn't certain what made her so suddenly volatile, either, unless it was hearing her former fiancé admit that he now regretted treating her like unclaimed freight. Or maybe it was having Derek, who was partially responsible for this entire fiasco in the first place, treat her as though *she* were guilty. "My private life is none of your business. And if it were . . . how dare you suggest I'd make time with another woman's fiancé— even though he once was mine!"

It would be smart to back off, he told himself. He'd had no right to call her on what had probably been a very innocent visit. But he was used to operating on instinct, and at the moment it told him Trey was having second thoughts about the woman that got away. Unfortunately neither Trey nor the woman knew she now belonged to Derek Cabot.

"Whoa," he said quietly, trying to placate her. "I'm concerned about how it looked to someone else. We're being watched on all sides, you know. Elizabeth is probably hanging out an upstairs window even as we speak."

"I don't believe you for a minute!" she shouted, obviously unimpressed with his reasonable approach. "I think you've taken on this job of pretending to be my husband like just another Farnsworth–Morreaux project. You want to bully me into operating your way, just like you did before. Well, I don't work for you anymore!"

Charlotte yanked the door open, anxious to escape from him and the confining little house. "I've been my own woman for a year," she said angrily, her hand on the doorknob, prepared to slam the door behind her, "and nothing's going to change that!"

She turned, her chin in the air—and spotted not only Bitsy and Darby, but several other members of the press whom Kendra had said would be coming and going all week.

She began to feel as though she were trapped in a Regency novel—except that instead of a parlor farce, this was a front porch farce. People came onstage, upset everything going on, then exited to make room for the next onstage disaster.

She stopped still, aware that her mouth hung open.

She vaguely registered footsteps behind her, then a strong, gentle hand moved up into her hair. Derek turned her toward him while the interested audience watched.

"I didn't mean that I don't want you to keep your shop," he crooned in a lover's voice. "I meant that I want us to have more time to spend together. Does that really deserve all this shouting?"

His eyes were inches from hers, his lips even closer than that. For an instant, she forgot what the problem was and lost herself in the tender magnetism that seduced her closer. She groped for reason. "I...you..."

"I know, I know," he said with disarming self-deprecation. "I'm very hardheaded and maybe sometimes you have to shout to be heard."

"You...accused me..."

"Of being a workaholic. I know. I'm sorry. It's just that I've been there, and now that we're married I don't want us to miss one precious moment together because one or the other of us is putting in overtime. Just give up working weekends, that's all I ask."

"Most weddings..." she said distractedly, resuming her role, "are on weekends."

"Then we'll have to coordinate days off during the week." He kissed her chastely, apologetically. "Come back inside and let's..." He paused to kiss her less chastely this time. Then he pretended to notice the press on the walk for the first time. His grin of embarrassment was frighteningly skillful.

"Ah, sorry," he said. "We...had a difference of opinion and now we're going to make up. Excuse us."

He pushed Charlotte through the doorway and closed the door behind them.

She slipped out of his spell with a thunk.

"And you call me a good actress," she said with the famous duchess's sarcasm. "If De Niro had seen that performance, he'd be worrying about the rest of his career. I begin to wonder just how often you've pretended to be some hapless woman's husband."

"This is the first time," he said, taking hold of her arm, "and I'm so good at it because the role of your lover seems to fit me very well. As well as it fits you to be mine."

"I would not be your lover if...!" Whatever the dire circumstances were that would never allow such an event were never spoken.

She was pulled into his arms and kissed into silence.

She drew back, shaken and confused. "Don't think that all you have to do is..."

He kissed her again, and this time she didn't even fight it, because at least he was right about that. The role of lovers did fit them well. They had yet to carry a kiss that far, but they'd certainly learned to make an art of the kiss itself.

As Charlotte clung to his neck, she felt something new in his arms. This was more than the physical dynamite usually generated whenever they touched, this kiss had a message.

He could have left her on the little porch to explain away her anger to the press collected on the walk. If she had been exposed for the liar he and Caroline had made her, the scandal would have attached itself to her, not to him, because of her history with Trey. She was sure Derek knew that. He had far less at stake here than she did, yet he'd come to her rescue.

Then she remembered that he'd always come to her rescue. When press releases had been late, he'd always been the one who stayed half the night in the office with her to get it together and get it right. He'd always grumbled about it, and reminded her that she'd have to move faster, but he'd seen her through it.

Because he cared? That possibility so stunned her that she pulled out of his arms and stared up at him. Then she saw it in his eyes. He did care. This was real.

"Oh, no," she whispered, as though someone had just handed her a cobra.

He knew precisely what had alarmed her. It had alarmed him, too, when he stopped to think about it. The trick was simply to feel and not analyze.

"I'm afraid so, Charlie," he confirmed with a grin. "You're in love with me."

She remained incredulous. "And you're in love with me."

"Yes."

"Well..." She uttered a little gasp of dismay and spread her arms, turning in exasperation. "Great." When she faced him again, she said irritably, "You know, this is all your fault. You entrap me in this big lie, you come on all charming and possessive and lure me into relaxing with you, then you spring *this* on me."

"*I* spring this?" he demanded, knowing it was critical that he didn't laugh. "I didn't do this by myself, you know. You're the one with eyes like the dawn and a backside that drives me wild. You're the one who melts every time I touch you, and who looks at me as though I'm the one thing in your life that's forbidden but that you want above all else."

She stared at him, startled, because that was precisely how she felt.

"You expect a man to not respond to that?"

She didn't have an answer. But she had to tell him where they stood. "Well, I, for one, am not doing this."

He raised an eyebrow. "You think you have a choice?"

"We all have choices. People fall in love and think they *have* to be drawn in by it, they have to lose their minds and their plans—provided they do get as far as the altar—and provided the other one doesn't leave them there." She studied him one more exasperated moment and marched off to the bedroom.

He followed her, noting in concern the defiant look in her eyes. When she pulled her suitcase out from under the bed, he knew he had to take control.

He sat on the edge of the bed and watched her prop the case open on it and turn to the chest of drawers.

"I'm out of here," she said. "I'm tired of Kendra's wedding controlling *my* life."

"You promised a lot of people you'd see this through," he reminded quietly.

"Big woo," she said flatly, tossing silky underthings at the suitcase. "Other people break promises and seem to get on just fine. People who know them don't even seem particularly disappointed in them. The sky does not fall."

"That's because..." A pair of black lace panties fell over the side of the suitcase. He picked them up and studied them. "There are some people you expect things from, and some people you know won't come through for you. When you learn to tell the difference, you don't get hurt."

She snatched the lacy scrap from him and slapped it into the case. "The same rules don't apply to everyone, is that what you're telling me? Do I see the male tendency to a double standard rearing its ugly head?"

"No. I'm trying to tell you as gently as I can that, for all your denials, you haven't recovered from what happened to you last year. And recovery is taking too long."

Fury and indignation warred for supremacy. She indulged them both by slamming the lid of the suitcase down and shoving it across the bed. "Like you know all about it!" she shouted at him.

"I know something about it," he returned mildly, "because I know you very well. You thought you'd found a kind and gentle man who was your ideal of the laid-back romantic. What you didn't realize was that he's laid-back because he's indecisive, and he seems romantic because the seductive gesture is easier than standing toe-to-toe with a woman and telling her what you can give and what you expect in return."

She walked away from him because he was absolutely right. She couldn't have put it into words, but she could see that was precisely what had happened.

"The trouble here is," he said, coming up behind her and placing his hands on her shoulders. She wasn't going to like this, but he was used to getting the broadside of her anger, and it had to be said, "That I think you truly are over Trey, but you haven't recovered from the fact that the Duchess of Winter made an error in judgment."

She spun around under his hands to look up at him, anger and pain bright in her eyes. He rubbed gently over the points of her shoulders in comfort if not apology.

"And it's become easier to pretend that it's a matter of trust, rather than a matter of self-doubt. You pretend that men in general—me in particular—aren't worthy of your trust, instead of admitting that you can't bear the thought of being wrong a second time."

She brought her arms up to break his hold and went to the window. She inhaled deeply of the scent of roses.

"My point is," he said, picking up a cosmetic bag that had fallen over the side of the bed, "that in my estimation Trey is a jerk and you don't owe him anything, and Elizabeth is like something out of Tennessee Williams who is interesting to watch but who the hell really cares what happens to her? But they're not the only ones who'd get hurt here if you storm out four days before the wedding and speculation and scandal take over."

She groaned and dropped her forehead on her arms folded on the sill. He pressed his advantage subtly, carefully.

"There are your parents, Caleb, Babs, Kendra. Am I wrong, or is she showing signs of being a real person?"

She didn't answer, but took another deep draft of air.

"Then you should consider all the things that would be said about you if you walk out now. They'll think you can't stand the sight of Trey and Kendra together, that you and I have quarrelled and that you can't keep your relationships together. Bitsy might try to talk to Caroline to find out what happened, and God knows how that would turn out."

"All right, all right!" Charlotte spun away from the window. She walked past him to the suitcase, dumped its contents into the middle of the bed, then slammed the case shut, locked it and tossed it under the bed.

She scooped up the undies and dropped them into the still-open drawer, then closed it with a bang. She turned to face him, temper and hurt feelings in her eyes.

"You're absolutely right about me," she said. "I hate being stupid. And I'm not going to do it again."

He grinned and leaned back against the dresser, bracing his hands on the surface on either side of him. "You'd have to be dead to assure yourself of that. You're only human, Duchess. Emotion overrode intelligence. It happens to the best of us."

"Has it happened to you?" she challenged.

He nodded, his gaze snaring hers. "It's happening to me right now. I've been just a little in love with you since the night we stayed up to get the videophone press release out on time." He sighed with resignation. "It became terminal when you almost hit me behind your father's house in your classic tank. I know it isn't smart, but I'm not running away from it."

"Of course not. You love to rise to the challenge, test your endurance, push the limits of mind and body. I just want to help other people have nice weddings."

"To make up for not having one yourself."

Charlotte expelled a frustrated breath and went to the closet where she'd stored the plum-colored bridesmaid's dress.

"We're talking in circles," she said, pulling out the plastic bag looped over the hanger of the last dress to be altered. It contained the half-finished cape. "And I have work to do."

"Fine." Derek straightened away from the dresser, shaking off the urge to throw her onto the bed and make her listen to him, then make love to her. Generally he was short on patience, but he could be long on finesse when he forced himself. "I'll put on the coffee."

"No," she said, sitting down at the sewing machine, squinting at the bright evening sunlight shining directly on her from the window. "Don't do anything thoughtful or sweet. Just let me be."

He went to draw the drape in direct defiance of her directive. He paused as he passed her chair to pinch her chin between his thumb and forefinger and raise her face to him.

"I'll do as I please, Duchess," he said. "And the only thing I will let you be is mine. Get used to it." And he walked away.

Chapter Six

Charlotte awoke with a vicious headache. The second cape had not gone well and she'd finally had to cut a new piece of tulle and start over. She'd worked until two in the morning, propped up by the coffeepot Derek had placed at her elbow before going to bed at midnight.

She slipped out of bed and into the mint-green cover that matched her flimsy peignoir and peeked into the living room. Derek was still asleep on the sofa. She wasn't surprised. She'd heard him tossing and turning until long after she'd finally turned out her light.

A desperate need for a cup of tea made her pad quietly into the kitchen and fill the kettle. Then she tiptoed across the carpet to peer out the window over the sofa. It was raining! In September in southern California that was unusual enough to make her stop and stare.

She went to the door and pulled it open, letting the slightly cooler air flow in. The mellow light filtering through the cloudy sky made her feel curiously melancholy.

This was the kind of day that defined romance—a moody sky, a couple huddled under an umbrella, stopping for lunch at a cozy café or running home to share it in a cozy nook.

I, she thought, *will get to share it with a lap full of silk flowers while I make headpieces for the bridesmaids.*

She was about to turn back to the kitchen when she noticed Bitsy and Elizabeth coming down the walk.

No. Please. Not this morning. Not with Derek still asleep on the sofa where he'd obviously spent the night rather than in her bed.

She wasn't sure what told her they wouldn't be taking the turn to the guest house where the press was staying, but she knew they were coming here.

She raced to the sofa, grabbed Derek's shoulder in both hands and shook him.

DEREK CAME AWAKE with the sincere conviction that he was caught in a clothes dryer. A very strong force buffeted him back and forth, and when he tried to sit up to evaluate his situation, the blanket was ripped from under him, rolling him onto his back.

"God!" he groaned, falling back against his pillow only to thunk his head against the arm of the sofa. His pillow had also been confiscated by the throttling force.

Confused and woozy, but determined not to be taken without a fight, he swung his legs over the side of the sofa. A fast-moving something in green silk landed in his lap, forcing him back down. Arms circled his neck, lips found his mouth and kissed him to complete wakefulness.

For a moment Derek thought he'd been caught in a time warp. This resembled in close detail a dream he'd entertained on a nightly basis when he'd been about fourteen.

Then he realized that he was caught in a web of straight blond hair and flower-garden perfume. He didn't know how to explain Charlotte's behavior, but made a swift decision on the spot and quickly capitulated on the previous one.

He didn't *care* what had prompted her change of heart, and he would gladly be taken however the hell she wanted to take him.

"Charlotte? Derek? Kids, yoo-hoo!"

The delicious little fantasy crashed around his ears. He recognized the voice at the door as Bitsy's and understood exactly what had happened.

He wasn't sure why the truth annoyed him so completely. They'd been playing games for the benefit of the Farnsworths and the press since the moment Caroline had made her fateful announcement. He supposed it was because he'd been half-asleep and vulnerable and easily convinced that Charlotte's sudden ardor had been real.

Understanding how he felt didn't lessen the annoyance, however. And he felt the need to deliver a payback.

Charlotte tried to slip off his knees to answer the screen door through which both women peered.

But instead of letting her go, he stood, tossed her over his shoulder and went to the door himself.

"Derek!" Charlotte whispered angrily, pounding one fist on his back.

He ignored her.

"Good morning," he said to the two stunned faces in the doorway. He gently swatted the hip on his shoulder. "Sorry. She gets difficult sometimes and the only way to deal with her is to take away her choices." Then he leaned down and let Charlotte slide until her feet hit the carpeting. "Look, Charlie," he said with good humor. "Guests. Come in, ladies."

He opened the door as Charlotte stood aside, impotent with surprise at his audacity, affected, despite her fluster, by the bare-chested sight of him in cotton pajama bottoms.

"Sounds like the kettle's boiling," he said. "Good timing."

"I'm sorry," Bitsy said in a tone that sounded anything but. Charlotte could see her eyes dancing with the prospect of the first few paragraphs of her next column. Cabots Prefer Rough Stuff Behind Closed Doors. Read On For Details. "But I hadn't realized you were making alterations to the bridesmaids' dresses. I promised the fashion page I'd reshoot for them. Elizabeth said you have the dresses here."

Charlotte's professional self came to the fore, a circumstance she thought fortunate since her personal self was flustered and unable to cope.

Graciously she brought the dress out while explaining about the addition of the cape.

"The headpieces are floral garlands, but I haven't put those together yet."

Elizabeth frowned. "When do you think you'll have one for Bitsy to photograph?"

"I'll have to be certain Kendra and the wedding party approve first," Charlotte replied. "But I should have one ready by dinner tonight."

"Fine. Shoes and bouquets will remain the same?"

Charlotte shook her head. "Shoes will, but the girls had intended to carry a single calla lily—elegant but stark. Now they'll carry old-fashioned nosegays in the deep colors of the headpieces."

Bitsy hastily made notes. Then she looked up as Derek came back into the room with a tray of cups and a steaming teapot. He'd also bowed to propriety and put on his pajama top. Bitsy looked disappointed.

Derek presided charmingly over tea, pulling Charlotte into his arm when she sat beside him on the sofa. Even Elizabeth seemed to relax. Slowly but surely, Charlotte realized, he was convincing them that the loving, sparring, playful couple he and she pretended to be was real.

But when their guests left, Elizabeth carrying the dress over her arm, Derek's charm evaporated into a curious, moody quiet. He helped her clear away cups, then excused himself to shower and change for a mid-morning meeting in Caleb's study. The uncharacteristic mood so surprised her that she swallowed her complaint about being thrown over his shoulder like an old bolt of fabric.

A quarter of an hour later he came out of the bedroom in light pants and a soft gray pullover. In his quiet mood, he looked like a stormy study of man in monochrome. His angles seemed sharper, his features darker, his height and breadth dramatically exaggerated.

He made her feel curiously out of tune, out of place. She didn't like it.

"Something wrong?" she asked as he went to the end table where he'd left his watch.

He gave her a quick, cool glance as he slipped on the expansion band. "Strange question," he replied. "I thought in your estimation everything was wrong."

She considered whether or not to pursue this. But this was a side of him she'd never seen, and there was a challenge inherent in being kept at arm's length—particularly when she remembered what it was like to be *in* his arms.

"I meant with you, not with the situation," she replied quietly, fiddling with one of the silk flowers strewn around her on the sofa. "It's unlike you to be so...remote."

He raised a mocking eyebrow. "You asked me last night to let you be. This is what it's like."

She didn't like it. It occurred to her that this didn't make sense when she had indeed asked for it, but it didn't seem to matter.

"You told me you would do what you pleased."

"Maybe it pleases me," he said, "to let you be. God knows it has to be easier than trying to figure you out."

"I wasn't aware," she said a little stiffly, "that I was that complicated."

He snatched up a ring of keys near where the watch had been and gave them a thoughtful toss. "Maybe I'm the one who's grown complicated. Maybe I don't like to wake up with a woman in my arms and discover she's there as part of the script."

He dropped the keys in his pocket and reached for the doorknob.

That brought her to her feet. "Wait a minute!" She approached him, hands on her hips. He rolled his eyes and waited.

"Do you mean to tell me," she said slowly, "that you're angry with me because I tried to save the charade this morning just as you've done half a dozen times since this all started? Would you have preferred that I let the ladies find you asleep on the sofa and give them proof that we aren't sleeping together? That we aren't married? That we can hardly exchange a civil word?"

She was right, of course, and that somehow made it worse. He had no idea what was happening. He never acted on emotion. Even when his feelings were involved, he made decisions based on logic—in business and with women.

But this woman had scrambled his brain. He wanted her desperately, even knowing he'd probably never have a moment's peace with her. And here he was, acting like an outraged boy because he'd misread a move she'd had little choice in making. He couldn't explain it.

He pulled the door open. "I'll see you at dinner in the big house," he said, and closed the door behind him.

CHARLOTTE'S HEADACHE had reached colossal proportions by early afternoon. She tried another cup of tea, a small bowl of soup, several aspirin, but nothing worked.

Paradoxically, the headpiece was coming together beautifully. The roses combined gracefully with the five-petaled little flower and the baby's breath to create a fanciful, romantic wreath. The tiny pearls, looped delicately in scallops around the circle, gave the flowers a touch of elegance.

Charlotte placed the wreath on her pounding head and peered into the mirror. She frowned when she saw that the silk stood up stiffly, without the naturally relaxed inclination of real flower petals.

She pondered the problem. Steaming would do it, she thought. The small appliance used to loosen wrinkles from fabric would be ideal. But her steamer was at the shop and the thought of driving on the freeway with her headache seemed too enormous a task. All she wanted was to take a hot bath and a nap.

Then it occurred to her. The steam from a hot bath would be just as effective as a steamer to assure her that it would do what she hoped.

Filling the tub with hot water, Charlotte pulled off the robe she'd never changed out of, placed the coronet of silk flowers on her head, and climbed into the bathtub.

She muttered a little cry as she displaced the steamy water, then rested her head back against the inflatable pillow. The ends of her hair dragged in the water, but she didn't care. Tying it back would have compounded her headache.

As the hot water began to soothe her tense muscles, Charlotte rested her arms on the side of the tub, and crossed her feet on the waterspout. She closed her eyes and tried to analyze Derek's behavior that morning.

Nothing computed. She'd tried over and over again throughout the day to find a reason for his sudden distance and couldn't. She went over everything that had happened, and everything they'd said to each other.

Then, in the quiet of her little self-created steam room something came together in her mind. "Maybe I don't like to wake up with a woman in my arms," he'd said, "and discover she's there as part of the script."

Her mind played over her frantic reaction when she'd spotted Elizabeth and Bitsy on the path, the way she'd torn the blankets from him and leaped on him when she saw the women try to peer through the screen door.

He was angry because he'd awakened thinking she meant the kiss and the embrace, then discovered she'd done it as part of their loving couple act.

She groaned in the steamy, afternoon light. If you only knew, she thought, how easy it is to touch you, to kiss you, to let you hold me. If you only knew how much it makes me wish this wasn't an act, that we did have the right to be together.

"Oh, Derek." She groaned again with the knowledge that they were as different temperamentally as their cars, she reaching back into the past for happiness, he moving ahead, always forward, ever faster, in search of a new challenge, a new chancy endeavor.

DEREK WALKED INTO the guest house, aware instantly of the unusual silence. Then he heard the quiet splash of water, and a soft little groan. He followed the sounds in concern to the open bathroom door and stopped on the threshold, momentarily paralyzed by the sight that greeted him.

He knew he wasn't dreaming, because he could feel the wood of the doorway molding under his right hand, the warm mist of the steamy air against his face. He heard the gentle splash of the water in the bathtub, and the soft little sound from the woman in it. This had the texture of reality.

But he couldn't believe what he *saw*. Charlotte lay naked in the water from which steam rose and swirled. It was no surprise, of course, to find her naked in her bath, but he had difficulty determining the significance of the coronet of flowers in her hair. Then he decided it didn't need significance. It gave her the look of some exotic nymph performing her ablutions in a natural spring.

She was every bit as perfect as he had imagined. Water lapped against small, round breasts, pink and bead-tipped from the hot water. The narrow waist and the slight flare of hips were indistinct, but she raised languid arms beaded with moisture and he couldn't dispel the notion that she'd cast a spell.

Still unaware of him, she raised one leg out of the water, gracefully pointed her toe to stretch it, rotated her foot at the ankle, then dropped her leg back into the water with a splash and a sigh.

Then she struck him to the core of his being with a softly spoken, woebegone, "Oh, Derek."

He heard the need in it, and felt his own need respond. He moved into the room and she sat up, startled. When she realized it was him, the fear slowly left her eyes and a sweet resignation took its place.

"Hi," she said softly.

He sat on the edge of the tub, reaching across her to brace his hand on the other side of it. Steam rose up to coil them in its misty arms.

His eyes went over the fine structure of her chin and jaw, the bright pink of her cheeks, the glow in her eyes and the fine mist of steamy dew that covered her. He raised his gaze to the wreath of flowers in her hair and smiled.

"Is that how a duchess bathes?" he asked, his voice quiet and deep in the tiny room.

"It's the prototype for the wedding," she replied just above a whisper. "The flowers were stiff and I thought steaming them would help, but I didn't have my steamer with me. And I needed to soak. So..."

Of course. That was how she did things. If there was a relaxed, romantic way to accomplish something, she found it. The need to touch her became unbearable. He ran his index finger lightly across a flushed cheekbone. "I heard you say my name a moment ago," he said.

She nodded, the gesture fascinating him as the flowers tilted gracefully in her hair. "I'm sorry about this morning." Her eyes grew wide and dark and he felt himself drawn into their beckoning depths. "The kiss was real, even though I did it because Elizabeth and Bitsy were at the door." She shrugged a delicate, fine-boned shoulder. "In some weird way, I feel as though it's all real."

It was. He had to show her.

Derek stood, reached down to take her hands and pulled her to her feet. He took a thick gray towel from the rack, wrapped it around her and lifted her out of the tub.

Charlotte felt as though her heartbeat might strangle her. For a moment he continued to hold her. Her arms looped around his neck, she looked into his hot, dark eyes and felt her own desire erupt like a fountain.

She closed the half inch that separated their lips and opened her mouth over his. He kissed her hungrily, taunted her with his tongue, nipped at her bottom lip, dipped his head to plant a kiss on the bare flesh above her towel.

"Derek!" she breathed into the wiry crispness of his hair.

He heard the passion in her whisper and felt it fuel his own. He swung her to her feet, unwrapped the towel from around her and, holding it in both hands, secured her in one arm and buffed her back and hips dry with the other end of it.

Then he wrapped it around her from behind, pulled her back against him and rubbed slowly, gently, over her breasts and her stomach. He leaned over to pass the towel over her thighs and she turned in his arms to catch him in her warm and fragrant embrace.

She nipped his ear, kissed his cheek, then raised his face and looked into his eyes. Hers held a love that was easy to read, and a thousand mysteries he didn't understand.

His held a fathomless passion and possession so strong she knew she'd feel it even without his arms around her.

"This will change everything," she warned softly.

He ran his thumb over her bottom lip, concentrating on it a moment before he looked up again into her eyes. "No, it won't," he insisted. "It'll just reaffirm the truth. We belong to each other."

Then he tossed the towel aside, lifted her into his arms and walked into the bedroom.

Chapter Seven

Derek placed Charlotte in the middle of the bed, then went to the open window through which they could hear the sounds of laughter at the pool, the drone of bees in the rose garden and, from somewhere distant, the sound of a lawn mower.

He pulled the window closed and smiled at her as he came back to the bed.

"I've had enough of snoops. It's one thing when we're onstage..." He sat beside her and leaned over her, a serious frown replacing the smile as he framed her face in his hands. "But quite another—" he leaned down to kiss her tenderly "—when we finally have the opportunity to write the scene ourselves."

Then he fixed her with a smile that was both gentle and devilish.

She expected him to make some witty remark, some astute, sophisticated observation—but instead he just looked at her, a hand braced on either side of her on the mattress.

She ran both hands up the front of his sweater. "What are you thinking?" she asked.

He caught one hand and planted a kiss in its palm. "That you don't look like the haughty duchess at the moment." He ran a fingertip down the middle of her from her clavicle to her navel. "You look like some wicked little druid."

He took the coronet from her hair and reached up to put it carefully on the bedside table.

Charlotte felt that light strum of his finger awaken every nerve ending in her body. It was important, she thought, that he know who she really was.

"It's just me," she said, tracing the line of his jaw with her fingertips. "The woman who so frustrated you for a whole year because she had a tendency to look backward rather than forward, and because she tended to operate with a slowness that annoyed you." Her fingers moved over the sturdy square of his jaw. "You're sure you want to do this?"

Derek slipped a hand under her, splayed it against her back and brought her up with it to within an inch of his own body. Her wide eyes questioned him.

"I've watched you work," he said, kissing her forehead. "I understand your fascination with the past a little better." Then he tilted her sideways into his arm and cradled her there, running a hand gently down the smooth flesh of her side and over her hip. "And some things," he said, lowering his voice intimately, "are done best when they're done slowly."

And then it began, the languidly deliberate exploration of every little inch of her body, every plane of it and every secret shadow.

Charlotte, aroused by his possessive touch and his reverent fascination, felt desire ignite as his hands moved over her, learning every little detail, she was sure, and even a few secrets her heart held.

He charted her breasts with a slowness that reduced her to absolute stillness.

When he put his mouth to the pearled tips of her, she felt it draw up the dignity she'd tried to reserve, the control she'd unconsciously tried to maintain.

"Derek!" she whispered as she struggled to retain at least one protective mechanism.

But he was drawing a line of kisses down the middle of her body, over her stomach, to the juncture of her thighs.

Flame licked at her with the tip of his tongue and caution shredded and fled in the fingers with which she gripped her pillow.

She was aware first of a sense of surprise that it made her feel free rather than vulnerable.

Then she realized what freedom did for one. Her body trembled on the very edge of infinity, then flung her out without fetters of any kind.

She'd never experienced that before. She'd always remained partially connected, at least some thread of reality caught in her grasp and anchoring her.

But this time she was soaring free, as though the vastness of what she felt needed the eternal space of forever. But then she became aware of being there alone.

"Derek."

She said his name softly, but he heard the edge of wonder in it. She groped for him, as though not sure where she was.

"Here," he said, lying down beside her and enfolding her in his arms. "Right here."

He expected her to need to lie still for a moment, to ground herself. But he'd apparently mistaken her purpose when she reached for him. She hadn't needed him to reassure her; she'd wanted to take him with her.

She knelt beside him and slipped her fingers up under his sweater, traced the hem of his undershirt to the barrier of his slacks and tugged to release it.

He let her work over him without trying to help, enjoying the seriousness of her concentration, the feverish flush on her cheeks.

The undershirt free, she knelt astride him, slipped both hands under him and tried to lift him to a sitting position as he'd done to her. Without his help, she found it impossible.

She gave him a sweet, scolding look. "Are you going to help me?"

He lay passive, thinking nothing had felt this delicious in recent memory. Even past memory.

"I want to see your next move," he said shamelessly.

Still astride him, she sat back, almost ruining the slim chance he had of remaining in control of his body long enough to see what direction her resourceful mind would take.

She raised an eyebrow and he caught a glimpse of the duchess. He felt a trepidation that called to that part of him that loved to flirt with danger.

Without a word, she unbuckled his belt, unzipped his slacks, and scooting backward over him, tugged on them.

The sensation that raged through him as she slid over him made him arch involuntarily, giving her just the advantage she needed to slide his slacks and briefs over his hips and off.

She came back to him, kneeling over him braced on her hands, and smiled with blatant self-satisfaction into his eyes. She had every right to it.

"That's the difference between us," she taunted softly, pausing to blow a warm breath across his chest. "You think every little detail done exactly to your specifications is so critical to the outcome of a project. But I prefer to explore the alternatives. There are other ways to get things done than by the charge-ahead means you always choose."

That gentle scolding administered, she tried to scoot backward again, intent on showing him just how inventive she could be.

But he had plans of his own. And a desperation he'd never known before.

He sat up to yank off the sweater and shirt, tossed them over the edge of the bed, then lifted her at the waist and lay back, placing her precisely where he wanted her.

He slipped into her and her body welcomed him with the ease of two people made for each other. He plunged deeply and she leaned to accommodate him, bracing on the hands they laced together between them.

He watched the little pleat form between her eyes that accompanied a little gasp of pleasure. Then she smiled at him with a helpless little inclination of her head that said what he already knew—there wasn't a word for how this felt, for how perfect, how all-pervading it was. It went deeper even than his body probed inside hers. It touched everywhere, everything.

Then urgency made him unable to concentrate on anything but the demands of their connection. He began to move under her and she leaned in counterpoint. Swaying together, following the paths of two separate but concentric circles, they turned on the pivotal point of a shared desire—and a shared love.

The knowledge, now irrefutable, broke over both of them the same moment fulfillment did, releasing them from everything that held love back or down, freeing them from all but each other.

CHARLOTTE STRETCHED languidly the length of Derek's warm body, then let her head fall back against his chest with a contented sigh.

"We really should stop this," she said, planting a kiss in the mat of hair under her cheek, "and get dressed for dinner."

Derek felt too replete to move. "Man does not live by bread alone," he philosophized drowsily.

Charlotte laughed against him. "Whoever said that hadn't seen Babs's sourdough starter." She sighed again. "If only someone would deliver dinner here so that we could eat it in bed."

"That's almost too hedonistic to contemplate."

"Or we could pack it into a basket with a bottle of chardonnay, put the basket in my Duesenberg and drive to Monterey."

"Your Duesenberg is in three pieces at the moment," he reminded.

She groaned. "That's right. And a picnic basket wouldn't fit into your Porsche. So I guess we have to go to dinner."

He shifted, holding her closer. "Let's not. I'll bet they won't even miss us."

She nuzzled closer. "I promised to have one of the coronets ready to show Kendra tonight. Bitsy's anxious to photograph them."

The mention of the coronets reminded him of the almost mythical way this entire afternoon had begun. And that reminded him that he would never get enough of her. Already the feeling of satiation was being replaced by a gnawing, growing need.

"If you insist," he said, rolling to turn her onto her back. "But I'll need a memory of this afternoon to see me through the wedding party's giggles, Elizabeth's endless discussion of details and Trey's longing looks at you."

"I believe," she said, halfheartedly pushing him away, "that you've collected three memories already. Or was that four? I think I fainted on you the last time."

"I'd like to believe that, but I think you just fell asleep."

"Well, I hadn't had much to eat...."

He cupped a hand under her hip and the other under her back to break her ineffectual resistance. "We're back to that again, are we? Well, the sooner you cooperate, the sooner we'll go to dinner."

She gave him a dramatic, long-suffering sigh. "Oh, all right. If you have to have it your way...."

His way, she decided an instant later, was rather wonderful.

ELIZABETH DID NOT censure them when they arrived twenty minutes late for dinner. She didn't have to. She simply turned to the butler, who appeared at her elbow, and said with a regal flick of her hand, "You may finally serve dinner, Chadwick."

"Yes, ma'am."

Everyone gathered in the living room studied Charlotte and Derek speculatively. Charlotte was sure that to anyone who knew her well, the events of the afternoon showed on her face.

She'd seen the difference in the mirror as she applied her makeup, though she couldn't have described it. Something subtle about her had changed.

Despite the carefully applied eye shadow, her eyes looked wide and mystified, and her carefully outlined and painted lips, the same berry as her short, full-skirted dress, had a tendency to smile without reason.

Derek, looking into the mirror over her shoulder to knot his tie, smiled at her puzzled expression.

"I look," she said with a confused little shrug, "like my own country cousin."

He had dipped his head to study her, a very masculine smile curving his lips. Then he placed a light kiss on the side of her neck. "The duchess," he said, "is gone."

Charlotte was saved from the varied but merciless inspections when Kendra approached her, pointing to the paper bag she held in her hands.

"Is that the headpiece?" she asked anxiously.

"Oh! Yes. Briane?" Charlotte, Kendra, Briane and Denise converged on the mirror over a Queen Anne table. Charlotte placed the coronet on Briane's hair and stepped back to let Kendra examine it.

As they decided unanimously that it was perfect, Denise took it from Briane and tried it on.

"It has every subtle shade," Kendra marveled. "And the pearls are a nice, romantic touch." She put a hand to Charlotte's arm and squeezed gently. "You've come through again. I'm going to have the most devastatingly gorgeous attendants any bride every had."

It wasn't until they were seated at the table that Charlotte realized Trey was absent.

"Isn't Trey joining us for dinner?" Caleb asked, noting the empty chair.

"He wasn't feeling well this afternoon," Kendra explained, grinning at her friends. "He hasn't quite recovered from all the stingers he had at the Karaoke bar. He's napping."

Caleb looked at Edward as though to suggest that the current generation hadn't their stamina or their capacity to party.

Caroline's knowing gaze swung from Charlotte to Derek, then settled on Charlotte again with a dazzling smile.

Charlotte looked away, afraid to think it could all be so easy. Any moment the glow would wear off and she'd probably ask herself why she'd been so impulsive and so impractical.

Then Derek, seated across from her, smiled at her with their new intimacy in his eyes, and she truly wondered if it could ever be a valid question.

Babs helped Pauline serve again. As Charlotte bit into the succulent shrimp cocktail, she looked up to catch Derek's eye. He gave her that look again that she was sure created a bright aura around her and made hot color flood her face.

Dessert was Babs's cake served with a whipped-cream frosting. Everyone raved, including Kendra.

"This *is* delicious, Grandma," she said, studying the morsel on her fork. "And it's very pretty." She turned to Elizabeth. "Mother, couldn't we have this instead of the bakery cake? It would be even better tasting, and in keeping with the Victorian theme."

"The cake is ordered," Elizabeth said. "Bitsy has photographed the bakery's model topped with your crystal lovebirds."

"But couldn't we . . ."

Elizabeth sighed. "Kendra, you've already caused everyone enough trouble, first rejecting Jean Michel's dress, then forcing me to move heaven and earth to find another dress and change everything else to coincide.''

Charlotte saw Caroline's eyebrows go up as her glance turned in Charlotte's direction.

Charlotte bit back a wry grin. It was interesting that Elizabeth considered herself the one inconvenienced.

The gathering dispersed after dinner—Kendra and her attendants upstairs where Briane could try on the headpiece with her dress, and Babs to the kitchen with Pauline where she felt most comfortable. Elizabeth went off to her bedroom office to tie up some detail of the reception, and Caleb, Caroline, Derek, Charlotte and Edward relaxed in the living room to sip brandy and talk about the tickets Caleb had bought the soon-to-be newlyweds for their honeymoon in Tahiti.

Then he drew out another folder and passed it to Derek, who sat on the arm of Charlotte's chair.

Derek put his glass down and frowned. ''What is this?''

Caleb cleared his throat and blustered. ''Nothing much. Just something to make up for having your honeymoon interrupted because of my daughter's wedding.''

A blush of guilt flooding her face, Charlotte watched Derek's long fingers open the folder. He pulled out a pair of airline tickets and shot Charlotte a warning glance before saying with pleased surprise, ''Tickets to Paris. Caleb, this isn't necessary.''

Caleb looked embarrassed. ''Didn't want to send you to Tahiti,'' he said with a dry twist of his lips. ''Didn't think you'd want to bump into Kendra and

Trey when you finally got to get away. Caroline assured me Paris is one of Charlotte's favorite places.''

Charlotte knew she looked stricken. Derek leaned down to hug her as though sharing her surprise and whispered quietly, "Stop it. Do you want to hurt his feelings? It's going to be all right."

Charlotte made herself smile and thank him with a stunned courtesy Caleb seemed to find completely convincing.

"I brought some brochures home," Caleb said, patting his pockets. "What did I do with them? Oh, yes. I left them in the study." He groaned at the prospect of pushing his portly girth out of the deep chair. "I keep thinking I should get one of those chairs that throws you to your feet, but I can't help but wonder what happens if you miss."

Everyone laughed. Charlotte stood, desperately needing a moment alone. "Let me get them for you, Caleb," she said. "I was just going to see if there was any coffee left, anyway."

Derek gave her a look that was part concern, part warning. She patted his cheek.

"Be right back."

"On my desk," Caleb called after her.

Charlotte went directly to the study across the hall, the story about the coffee was nothing but a gambit to explain her eagerness to get away. She closed the big oak doors behind her and leaned against them in the dark.

She put a hand to her chest where her heart fluttered. Tickets to Paris. An expensive gift invested in gratitude for the disruption of a honeymoon that had never existed in the first place.

She was torn between thinking things had gone too far, and thinking they'd finally gotten to the point where they should be. After all the role-playing, she and Derek were truly in love, but that seemed to make it more difficult rather than easier to carry on the charade.

Confused by that thought, she groped along the wall for the light switch, but encountered nothing but the feel of genuine wood paneling. She turned to the other side of the door—and was stopped dead by a furtive sound behind her. A hand to the wall to retain her bearings, she stood still and listened.

She heard more movement, the rustle of clothing, what sounded like a stifled breath. Before alarm could take hold of her, she told herself reasonably that she was in a house filled with people that was located within a locked gate. This could not be an intruder. But who was it?

"Hello?" she said cautiously.

There was another long, pulsing silence, then more quiet movements.

Now a little worried, she inched toward the door. "Who's there?" she demanded in a firm voice.

There was another instant's silence, then a low, seductive voice came out of the dark. "It's me, Charlie."

"Trey!" she said with relief. For an instant, the quality of his voice hadn't registered, only the familiar sound of it. "What on earth are you doing here?"

Then she remembered Kendra saying he was napping to get over a headache. When he didn't answer her question, she remembered also how his voice had sounded—predatory and vaguely reckless.

"Oh, Charlie," he said, his voice even deeper, thicker than before. A hand caught hers in the dark and drew her farther into the room.

"Trey," she said, finally understanding what was happening, trying to draw her hand away. "Trey, stop it. What's the matter with you?"

"You know what the matter is." Suddenly his voice was in her ear and his arms were around her, taut with emotion barely held in check. She felt moist lips against her cheek and knew he'd missed her lips because she was tossing her head, pushing against him.

"Stop this right now!" she whispered harshly. "Your fiancée is just upstairs and her father is just across the hall!" She added belatedly, "Along with my husband!"

"Charlie, this is all wrong and you know it," he whispered urgently against her cheekbone, having missed her mouth again.

"You're damn right, it's wrong!" She tried to kick him and missed, pushed against him with all her might, but he was unusually strong in his ardor.

"I don't mean *this*," he said, finally zeroing in on her mouth and kissing her. She kept her mouth closed stubbornly as she continued to push at him. Revulsion and fury washed over her. "I mean the way it's ending up, you with Cabot, me with Kendra. She's more beautiful than you are, and she's more amenable, but she isn't you."

"Trey, you're supposed to marry her in two days!"

"I can't."

And that was what finally gave her the strength to shove him away. There was a gasp of alarm from him as he fell backward, then a scream from her as he caught at her skirt and took her with him.

She felt pain as her thigh collided with something hard and angular, then her shoulder knocked against the same object as she fell against it. There was the sound of furniture falling and glass breaking. She landed on something that expelled a loud, "Ooof!"

Darkness and surprise disoriented her. As she tried to recover, there was another crash. The study door burst open and someone flipped on the light. It glared harshly over the condemning little tableau on the floor.

A globe on a floor stand lay on its side, the meridian still rocking, the globe within it still spinning on its poles pins. The falling globe had collided with a glass-topped coffee table and knocked it over. The glass had cracked, and a fluted crystal dish lay overturned, little foil wrapped candies spewed all over the tweedy brown carpet.

Charlotte and Trey lay in a tangle among the legs of the coffee table. Trey was on the bottom, his head against the uppermost leg, his own legs trapped between the two legs on the other end of the table. Charlotte was draped across him, her dress hiked up to her thighs.

She pushed against the side of the coffee table to squint up at the door and found almost everyone in the household there.

Derek and her father made up the front row, both staring at her in confusion and concern. Behind them were Caleb and Caroline, also staring. Caroline had a hand to her mouth. Kendra and her attendants were behind them, Kendra coming around the little crowd to peer in openmouthed dismay at the compromising scene. Elizabeth arrived with a gasp of dismay.

Charlotte put a hand to her spinning head and groaned. Trey exacerbated the situation by reaching up to put a hand to her face. "You okay, Charlie?" he asked solicitously.

Then everyone was galvanized into action. Derek came forward to pull Charlotte to her feet, Edward and Caleb helping Trey.

Charlotte, still trembling a little, looked into the controlled temper in Derek's dark eyes and explained inanely, "I was looking for the light."

"Light switches are usually found against the wall," Elizabeth said, studying the disorder on the floor.

Even to Charlotte's own ear, the claim sounded like a lie. And when she blushed, she was sure it looked like a lie.

She turned to Trey, daring him to extricate them from this embarrassing scene. Whatever notion she might have had that he'd assume all blame to save her dissolved when he cleared his throat.

"I was asleep on the sofa," he said, grinning at Kendra who was looking at him with open suspicion.

"She just fell over me." He turned to Charlotte in all apparent innocence and asked, "What were you doing in here, anyway?"

Charlotte wondered how often she herself had fallen for that charmingly embarrassed smile. Who could be angry with anyone who looked so vulnerable and innocent?

It occurred to her to tell the truth. But her mind asked with a hint of gallows humor, *Why start now?* And if anyone should reveal the truth, it should be Trey.

"I'm sorry about the table, Elizabeth," Charlotte said wearily. She wanted desperately to extricate herself from this wedding and go home. She longed for the quiet, simple life she'd lived in her old North Hollywood home before this had all begun. "I'll have the glass replaced."

"Don't be silly," Caleb said when his wife righted her wounded table in obvious displeasure. "Are you all right?"

Caroline came to put an arm around her. "You should sit down, Charlie. You don't look well."

"I'm fine," she said. "But I'd like to go back to the guest house, if you'll all excuse me."

"I'll make you a cup of tea," Caroline offered.

Edward frowned into her eyes. "You don't look fine. Did you hit your head?"

"No." Charlotte shook it and immediately regretted it. The headache with which she'd begun the day was back with a vengeance. The intervening time, she thought, had certainly been eventful.

"I'm sure it would help her to get off her feet," Derek said, sweeping her up into his arms to do precisely that. "I'll take care of her, Caroline."

Charlotte was happy to lean her face against his shoulder and close her eyes as he negotiated the gauntlet of the suspicious audience and left the big house.

He said nothing as he carried her through the fragrant darkness and up the well-lit path to the guest house. At the door, he braced a knee against the wall and rested her on it while he retrieved his key.

Then they were inside, and he was putting her down in the middle of the bed. It reminded her of how he'd done that very thing only hours ago, and the lovemaking that had resulted and changed something vital within her.

"Stay still," he said, slipping off her shoes. "I'll put the kettle on."

He left the room in darkness, but put on the hallway light. She heard him at work in the kitchen, then his footsteps as he returned to the bedroom. He tossed his jacket at the chair and came to sit on the edge of the bed beside her.

"Are you really all right?" he asked, pulling the other side of the bedspread over her.

"Yes," she replied, "except for a few bruises where I landed against the coffee table."

"Then what the hell happened?" he asked. "I thought it was over between you, yet I keep finding you together."

She tossed the spread off and sat up. "It *is* over between us," she said angrily, her temper and her composure in shreds. She snatched the pillow from beside her and held it threateningly, "And if you dare suggest that what happened in the study was the result of some... some rendezvous... I'll..."

He took the pillow from her, tossed it behind her and pushed her gently back against it. "Then what happened?" he insisted.

She yanked the spread back over her, angry, disappointed and depressed.

"He kissed me," she said simply.

Derek reached over to turn on the bedside lamp. It cast a small puddle of light over the two of them.

"What?" he asked ominously.

"He was sleeping off the headache Kendra mentioned at dinner. Only she didn't mention he was doing it in the study. I blundered in in the dark, he woke up and heard me, and... and I guess he was probably..." She groped for a kind explanation. "You know, feeling last-minute panic, and maybe some leftover guilt from leaving me at the altar and..."

"You're telling me," Derek suggested dryly, "that he kissed you to make up for abandoning you in a church filled with people?"

Her look scolded him for deliberately misunderstanding. "No, I mean that when he gets panicky, he doesn't think straight."

"When he gets panicky," Derek amended, "he does whatever it takes to save himself."

She leaned into the pillow with a sigh. "Yes, I know. I shoved him away, he fell over the coffee table and grabbed for me as he went down. That's how we ended up... all entangled."

"No one believed his lame story for a minute. 'I was asleep and she fell over me.' He may as well have said, 'We fell off the sofa in the throes of passion.' Why didn't you say something?"

She winced as her head throbbed. "Because Kendra was standing right behind you."

"You don't think she has the right to know her fiancé was kissing his old flame?"

"I don't know." She rubbed between her eyebrows. "Maybe he really does love her, but he's just being a jerk. I fell in love with him because he was sensitive and sweet in a world filled with ruthless, hard-driving men." She cast him a glance that lumped him in their number. "Then the morning of our wedding, the only thing that arrived at the church was a messenger with a note from him that said he couldn't go through with it because he knew he'd fail me one day. He was probably right, because I'd have expected something from him. I'm not sure Kendra does. He's handsome and smart and her family likes him—that's the standard by which she's been brought up. She doesn't need anything for her personal self. They could probably make each other happy."

The kettle whistled and Derek answered its call with a profane, insightful observation.

He was back in a moment with two steaming mugs. He handed her one, then resumed his place on the edge of the bed. She scooted sideways and patted the place beside her.

"Want to sit with me?"

He did and he didn't. He was still full of angry, jealous questions, observations he'd like to make about the handsome, perennial fiancé. But Charlotte looked pale and tired, and there was evidence in her eyes that the episode with Prentiss had upset her. He put his cup down on the table and slipped into the small space she'd left him.

She leaned her head against his shoulder and sighed. "At least with a man who's straightforward, you know what to expect. You know the limits of the relationship."

He wasn't sure he liked the way that sounded. "You've found limits in our relationship already?"

She raised her head to sip her tea, then rested it against him again. "Well, you know. You're very open about thinking my involvement with the past is silly and a little weird. I like to wander around while you bulldoze ahead, and I'm always looking for the sweet little things you don't even notice. There'll be a lot we won't be able to share. But at least I know that. You haven't pretended to be one thing and turned out to be another."

He frowned into the shadows beyond their little pool of light. "It's a rule that opposites attract," he reasoned. "What results from two people who are very different is a healthy balance."

She was silent for a moment. Then she put her cup aside and lifted his arm to place it around her. She found a comfortable spot on his chest and closed her eyes.

"Right," she said, too belatedly to convince him that she meant it.

Chapter Eight

"What's on your agenda for today?" Derek asked as he peered around the bathroom door, pulling a simple white sweater over his head.

Charlotte, stretched out in warm bathwater to soak away her bruises from the night before, smiled lazily as she watched his head emerge from the round neck.

She loved the serious, sturdy look of him that hid a sparkling sense of humor and a deep, hot passion. It occurred to her that the woman she was today would probably not even look twice at Trey Prentiss.

"I have to finish the other headpiece," she said, "and I had promised to pick up a pair of patterned stockings from my shop for Kendra to wear. Presuming she's still speaking to me."

Derek ran a hand through his hair to smooth it and moved into the humid little room.

"If you take any flack because of what happened last night," he warned, "*I'm* telling everyone the truth."

"Hopefully," Charlotte said calmly, "they'll all just think it wasn't half as bad as it looked. They might even believe I just fell over him."

"Looking for the light switch that was a good fifteen feet away?"

"You're not helping." She sat up and winced as the movement forced pressure against the bruise on the back of her shoulder.

"What's the matter?" he asked, coming to lean over her.

"Nothing serious. Just a few bruises from falling over the coffee table."

Derek looked at the angry red-and-purple blotch the size of a saucer on the slope of her shoulder and swore.

"God! Is that the only one you've got?"

Without warning or ceremony, he hauled her out of the water and checked her over. Ignoring her protests that she was fine, he found a purple welt on her thigh and one on her backside.

"That's it," he said. "It's time Prentiss and I had a man-to—"

She wrapped her arms around him, the touch of her warm, soaking body penetrating his clothing. "They're just bruises that'll fade in a day or two." Her wide eyes mesmerized him as they pleaded prettily. "And though they are his fault, we fell because I pushed him. Please don't spoil Kendra's wedding."

"Charlie, he . . ."

Her eyes fell to his lips and prevented them from moving coherently.

"I don't care about him," she whispered, running the tip of her tongue along his bottom lip. "I just want to think about us." Then her tongue parted his lips and he was lost.

He made love to her swiftly, responsively, wrestling her for control of the encounter, then gladly relinquishing it when she insisted with artful boldness. Then he rolled her over and made love to her again, retaining the initiative this time just to show her the scope of pleasure he wanted to offer.

He was twenty minutes late for the meeting in Caleb's office. With Charlotte in his bed, he thought, he was going to spend his life twenty minutes late for everything.

"YOU'RE SURE YOU don't mind taking the contracts to the office safe?" Edward asked Derek.

Caleb had already left the study in response to the butler's urgent message from Elizabeth, and Edward and Derek sat over cups of coffee that rested on the cracked glass top of the coffee table.

"Not at all," Derek assured him.

"You didn't have other plans for today?"

The question was innocent enough, but Derek had worked with Edward in one capacity or another for twelve years. It was his job to read between the lines of every contract and every conversation and evaluate the unspecified and the unspoken.

He grinned at his boss as he leaned over to pick up his cup. "I apologized for being late."

"The two of you have been late for everything."

"Your daughter doesn't respond to being rushed."

"My daughter is determined and strong-willed, but very gentle deep down, maybe even fragile." Edward smiled honestly. "I know you to be honest and fair, but hardheaded and ruthless. And I know she's fallen in love with you.''

Derek remembered her strong resistance to his overtures and, last night, her practical assessment of their situation—an assessment he didn't particularly agree with, but found excessively reasonable all the same.

''She's tougher than you realize, Edward,'' he said. He took a sip of the strong, hot coffee, then put it down, thinking how much he'd come to enjoy sharing tea with Charlotte. ''But you know I've never injured or broken a delicate deal. And I always see that everyone wins.''

Edward sighed, his expression growing thoughtful. ''But you're very young. I wonder if you realize how different women are from business.''

Derek nodded. ''There was a time when I used the same approach on both. But I learned the difference when Charlie worked for me. Don't worry. I'm far more reliable than Prentiss.''

Edward made a scornful sound. ''Tell me something I don't know. He ducked out of this morning's meeting on the pretext that the jeweler needed to see him. I think he just didn't want to face you. What the hell happened last night?''

Derek knew Charlotte wouldn't be pleased that he told her father, but there were some things on which she wasn't the final authority.

''He made a move on her while she was groping around in the dark. She shoved him, he grabbed for her and they fell over the coffee table.''

Edward's response was pithy and obscene.

"Precisely," Derek said. "But I'll have a talk with him when he comes back from the jeweler. Warn him what'll happen to his own family jewels if he isn't careful."

Edward laughed wickedly. "All right. See you at dinner."

IN A PAIR OF pink sweats appliquéd with roses, Charlotte went to answer the authoritative rap on the guesthouse door.

Caroline pushed her way in, a paper bag of something aromatic in her hands. "Point me to the kitchen," she said.

Charlotte complied, following her to lean in the narrow doorway while her stepmother found the still-half-full kettle, the tin of tea and a pair of mugs.

"I'll tell you up front," she said as she worked, "that your father sent me here to... to sort of... feel out the situation, so to speak." She looked up to wince apologetically. "Poor choice of words. To assess the situation, to see if you're... happy. Plates?"

Charlotte walked into the kitchen to pull down two.

"What's in the bag?"

Caroline opened it and removed two fat, fragrant croissants.

"Yum!" Charlotte said.

"And not only that, they're filled with raspberry. Should we skip the butter, or be truly decadent?"

As Charlotte considered, Caroline warned, "I'm going to be asking some tough questions."

Charlotte retrieved the butter from the refrigerator and led the way to the sofa.

Croissants halved and buttered and filling the small room with their aroma, Caroline tore off a bite of hers and sat back in her corner of the sofa.

"Okay. Spill your guts. Tell me everything. And give me details—your father will ask."

"You mean last night?"

"I mean Derek, and then last night."

Charlotte didn't want to answer questions, but she had to admire her stepmother's style. It was precisely this no-nonsense candor that had endeared her to Charlotte.

"Derek," Charlotte said, after chewing and swallowing her first bite, "is pretending to be my husband, remember? You wrote the play."

"Don't try to put me off with that," Caroline said, propping a designer loafer on the wicker tabletop. "Judging by the glow on the two of you, no one is pretending anything anymore. You've been intimate, haven't you?"

"Caro!"

She waved a bite of croissant helplessly. "Don't kill the messenger. Your father will ask."

Charlotte gave her a disbelieving glance as she reached for her tea. "I believe you're the one who's interested. Dad's always let me have my privacy."

"And so did I when you were in high school and relationships were a vast emotional experience. But those days are long gone now, Charlie."

Charlotte rolled her eyes over the rim of her cup.

"Oh, you know what I mean. You're still a young-ster, but you should be old enough to forget all your old traumas and know a good thing when you see it." Caroline put her croissant aside in order to study Charlotte carefully. "Do you?"

"I think so."

"So... are you?"

"What?"

"In love!" Caroline shouted impatiently. "Have you gotten over Trey? Are you out of your shell? Are you willing to try again with a man who makes Trey look like an adolescent?"

"Yes. Yes. Yes." Charlotte counted over all the questions, then added tardily, "Yes."

"Hallelujah!" Caroline leaned sideways to give her stepdaughter a hearty hug. "Thank God! I thought the way you were behaving in the beginning, you might blow the whole opportunity. He's perfect for you."

Charlotte shook her head as she put cup and crois-sant aside. "Actually, we agree on so little."

Caroline heaved a theatrical sigh. "Then you're meant for each other, my sweet, because that's mar-ried life in a nutshell."

Charlotte had to laugh. "Come on. Dad does abso-lutely everything you ask of him."

She agreed with a nod. "But only after he's said no, been forced to listen to my arguments, then been swayed by my brilliant oratory."

"I think that's called nagging."

"An ugly word for such inventive tactics. Has he mentioned marriage?"

"No, he hasn't mentioned marriage. We were only thrown together four or five days ago. We just..." She stopped, finding it difficult to make the admission in the face of Caroline's eagerness to hear it. "We're just getting to know each other."

Caroline shook her head at her as though she were simple. "He's been in love with you since your father brought him back from New York. And I think you were in love with him, but you were engaged to Trey. I believe that's what was behind the fireworks between you two—he thinks all things business, personal and financial should be handled the same, and when he couldn't deal with you that way, it made him angry.

"And you were drawn to him, intrigued by him, probably even felt something for him—but you were engaged to someone you thought was ideal, so it confused you. You took it out on yourself and everyone else in the vicinity."

Charlotte listened to the detailed analysis of that awful year just before she quit her father's company, and concluded that Caroline was probably right.

"That's all over now," she said, propping an elbow on the back of the sofa and frowning. "But the issue of Trey remains. Did Elizabeth or Kendra say anything to you about what happened last night?"

"No. I haven't seen Kendra all morning, and Elizabeth has been very much business as usual. What *did* happen?"

Briefly, undramatically, she related her encounter with Trey.

"You aren't serious!" Caroline exclaimed in shocked fascination. "Do you believe that young man? What did you do?"

"I shoved him. That's how we ended up entangled with the coffee table."

"Well." Serene again, Caroline took another sip of tea. "I'm sure Derek will take care of him, just as he's taken care of the table."

Charlotte lowered her hand. "What do you mean?"

"It was replaced by a new one this morning, just as I was coming over here."

"That isn't his responsibility."

"Of course it is. At least everyone will think it is. A responsible man makes good on his wife's charges and breakages." Caroline lowered her cup and said with a knowing glance, "And I imagine he's taking care of Trey Prentiss at this very moment."

DEREK HAD LITTLE TROUBLE finding Trey. Charlotte's ex-fiancé returned just as the furniture truck left with the damaged table. From the study window, he saw Trey slip around the back of the house and disappear into the garden and the tents being set up for the reception.

He found him sitting on the canvas bottom of the tent at the farthest end of the lawn. He leaned back on his hands, looking pensive and uncertain, his head thrown back as he stared at the ceiling of the tent. Derek supposed he might have looked poetic and tragic to someone who had patience with indecision and a lack of loyalty.

Derek walked into the shadowy interior. Trey sprang to his feet, taking a cautious step backward before he could stop himself. Then he seemed to force himself to relax and pretend he hadn't been avoiding him since breakfast.

"Good morning," Trey said with exaggerated cheer. "I was just going to check on Charlie. How is she this morning?"

"That's what I want to talk about," Derek said, wandering in his direction, hands in his pockets.

"Oh? She's all right, isn't she?"

"She's bruised," Derek said, stopping a few feet from him. He knew he didn't have to tell him whom he considered responsible.

"I didn't . . ." Trey began to protest.

"She told me what happened," Derek interrupted, slowly taking his hands out of his pockets. "She's bruised because she tried to get away from you and you brought her down when you fell."

"She shoved me."

Derek would have taken great satisfaction in hitting him just for that. He had no patience with people who couldn't relate cause and effect.

"Because you kissed her when she's married to me, and you're engaged to be married to someone else to-morrow."

Anger flared in Trey's eyes and Derek watched with interest, wondering if Trey was going to allow temper to overcome good sense. He hoped so.

"Charlotte and I had some good times. We share a history you can never be a part of, and you can't just blot it out by..."

Derek closed the small space left between them in two strides and resisted the impulse to grab him by his shirt collar and choke him.

"You listen to me," he said quietly, his arms loose and ready on the chance that he changed his mind about being reasonable. "You flatter yourself to think she remembers anything about you except the fact that you changed your mind about marrying her at the last minute and didn't even have the guts to show up in person and tell her."

He had to draw a breath, because the memory of that morning in the church infuriated him still.

Trey seemed unable to breathe even though he wasn't choking him.

"Even if she did consider she had a 'history' with you," Derek repeated the word scornfully, "I wouldn't give a damn about it. All I care about is her future, and that takes place with me. If you so much as come near the guest house before we leave, if you even speak to Charlotte in a crowd, much less try to see her alone, I'll grind you to powder, Prentiss.

"Now." He smiled pleasantly. "My advice would be that you don't do anything to scotch your relationship with Kendra, because that's the only thing that's saving your job at Farsnworth–Morreaux. Have a nice day."

Derek turned to leave and Trey took a step after him. Derek stopped and turned, halting him in his tracks.

Humiliated and angry, Trey said, "You're a bastard, Cabot!"

Derek nodded, his expression grim. "You'd do well to remember that."

"HE CHANGED HIS MIND, Henry," Charlotte was saying to Henry as Derek walked around the garages. "He's decided that was narrow-minded and chauvinistic and that I can drive the Porsche, after all. So please get me the keys."

Henry frowned, obviously torn between an unwillingness to deny a favorite guest anything, and a possessive, protective attitude toward the Porsche left in his care. Not to mention the promise he'd made to another favorite guest.

"He didn't tell me that, Mrs. Cabot," he said stoutly, his tall body blocking the open door at the end of the long bank of garages.

Charlotte, looking like a charming version of the duchess in a flowered dress and a broad-brimmed hat, said with the confidence of a beautiful woman to whom little is denied, "It was a recent decision. Reached just this morning, in fact. The keys, Henry."

"He didn't tell me," Henry repeated doggedly. "Why don't I drive you in the limo?"

"He went straight to a meeting in Mr. Farnsworth's study," she replied courteously. "Now I have to go to my shop to pick up a few important things for the wedding. I have a dozen stops to make and I wouldn't want to keep you out that long. You wouldn't want to be responsible for doing anything to make the wedding less than perfect?"

Taking pity on the poor man's dilemma, Derek made his presence known. Henry looked as though he'd been granted a death-row reprieve. Charlotte looked charmingly embarrassed, but only for a moment. She immediately turned her interesting technique on him.

"How would you like lunch at Dominick's?" she asked, knowing it was one of his favorite places.

"Followed by taking you shopping?" He handed Henry his briefcase. "Would you get the car, please, Henry?"

"Yes, sir."

As the chauffeur disappeared into the garage, Charlotte looked at Derek with disapproval. "You were eavesdropping."

Derek folded his arms, trying to hide the desire that rose swiftly in him at the sight of her, the terminal weakness he felt when she smiled at him, the memories of this morning brought back so sharply.

"I like to think of it," he said, "as studying tactics. Yours are truly amazing. One lie after another without so much as a blush or a flicker of an eyelash."

As the Porsche's motor growled to life, Charlotte moved out of its path to stand beside Derek. She smiled up into his eyes.

"*You* taught me to be an actress," she said.

He curled an arm around her waist and leaned over her upturned face. Greedily he watched the welcome in her eyes. "But you're not acting anymore, are you?"

She stood on tiptoe to close the gap and kiss him. "No," she said as Henry, in the Porsche, roared out of the garage in reverse. "I'm not. Are you?"

As Henry pretended not to watch, but polished the driver's side-view mirror with a rag from his pocket, Derek kissed her again to remind her what they'd shared and what still lay ahead of them after the demands of the day.

"Did that feel like acting?"

"No." She devoured him with her eyes one more moment, then smiled innocently. "Then you're not upset about the car?"

He turned her around and sent her toward it with a gentle swat. "Yes, I am. And just for that, you can drive."

"But... you'll be watching me. I'll be nervous."

"Just pretend I'm not here, and that Henry let you have the keys."

Henry looked in concern at Derek as he closed Charlotte into the driver's side.

"I came close to giving in, Mr. Cabot," he confessed. "You might consider giving Mrs. Cabot her own keys, or parking the Porsche at the Gables across the road." He pointed to the neighboring estate. "My conscience can't take being torn like this day after day."

Derek clapped his shoulder, then walked around the low-slung hood and leaped into the passenger seat without opening the door. "It's okay, Henry. This afternoon ought to settle the issue. Either she'll wreck it, or prove to me she's capable of driving it."

Henry looked doubtful of the outcome. "I'll see Chadwick has a brandy ready for you, just in case."

Chapter Nine

Charlotte had never expected to be seduced by power. It was against everything she stood for, everything she'd tried to sweep out of her life. But she was discovering that the power of a brilliantly designed, quickly responsive and maneuverable sports car was something else entirely.

Derek decided that letting Charlotte drive the Porsche was good for his character. Bad for his nerves, but good for his character.

Used to the steady solidity of her Duesenberg, Charlotte was quickly growing more confident with the Porsche's nimble responses. She drove faster than he did, changed lanes with abandon, found herself caught between one truck trying to pass another and floored the accelerator so that they shot out of the confining and potentially dangerous space like toothpaste from a tube.

"Remember," he said, trying to keep his voice calm, "that it isn't a motorcycle. And there's a cop somewhere in Beverly Hills who wasn't even impressed by Zsa Zsa."

She laughed and reached out to pat his knee. "Relax, husband," she said, heading for the fast lane. "This car is something else!"

He let his mind be distracted for an instant from the danger confronting the car he'd bought with his first substantial bonus, which symbolized his hard work and success, and with which he'd been through a lot, and concentrated on Charlotte's profile.

She had tossed her hat into the back and her platinum hair, which had been wound into a knot when they'd hit the freeway, was now streaming out behind her like a vapor trail.

"Do I detect the polluting encroachment of speed in my old-fashioned girl?" he asked.

She maneuvered around a slow compact. "Yes, I think so," she replied with no obvious regret. "It's fascinating isn't it, to be going fast and still feel in complete control?"

"I think that's a profoundly philosophical observation." He resisted covering his eyes when she slipped back into traffic just as it slowed to accommodate a truck changing lanes up ahead. She did it smoothly, easily, and he thought with surprise that he didn't know all there was to know about Charlotte Morreaux. "That's kind of what life's all about. Going as fast as you can while remaining in control."

"Now there's where we differ," she said. "I think life can only be enjoyed when you slow down to figure out what it's all about. Speed and power are a high, I'll admit it, but only for a little while. They make the scenery a blur. You can't say you've lived when you don't remember what life looked like. Uh-oh. That's my exit coming up.''

Derek looked over his shoulder. ''There's a pickup in the next lane that thinks it's a Ferrari. Please don't try to intimidate him into letting you in.''

Charlotte gave him a scolding grin. ''For someone who espouses the 'live hard, die young' philosophy, you certainly are jittery.''

''That's because you've got it wrong.'' He put a hand to the dash as she did just what he'd hoped she wouldn't do. With a wave and a kiss blown to the driver of the pickup, she slipped past him to take the next turn. ''The live hard part is right, but I intended to be doing wheelies in my walker. Charlie—damn it!''

There was the sound of brakes, and gears shifting down. Derek turned again to see just how close to death they were and was surprised when the driver shook his head tolerantly and blew the kiss back to Charlotte.

''See?'' she said, traffic roaring on as they turned onto the relative quiet of Camden Drive. ''If you're nice to people, they're nice to you. Want to have lunch before we shop? You look a little peaked.''

CHARLOTTE SAT on the edge of Mrs. Harmon's desk while Derek locked the finished contracts away.

Mrs. Harmon, Derek's secretary, who looked like Mayberry's Aunt Bea, operated like a high-powered brain trust, and had the sense of humor of a stand-up comic.

"Hmm," she observed with interest as Derek left them. "You two have finally seen the light?"

Charlotte pretended to misunderstand. "What light? I had to come to town and so did he."

"Really." The single word had a flat, disbelieving sound. "And that's why you're pretending to be husband and wife in a tiny little guest house?"

Charlotte gasped and looked around, returning a wave sent her way from far across the office. "How did you know about that?"

"Ginny in accounts payable told me."

Another gasp. "How did *she* know?"

"She had lunch with your mother the other day."

Charlotte groaned and put a hand to her eyes. "No. It's supposed to be a closely held secret. It just happened because . . ."

"I know, I know." Mrs. Harmon cut her off. "The shower. Caroline publicly announcing you'd been married and neglecting to secure a groom—and all this in front of Bitsy Tate. Fortunately Mr. Cabot saved her—and you."

Charlotte leaned toward her from her superior position, trying to look fierce. "You will not say a word to anyone, is that clear?"

Mrs. Harmon smiled beatifically. "Too late. KTLA called me. I'm going to be on the evening news."

For an instant, Charlotte wasn't sure whether or not to believe her. That was precisely the last chapter she'd envisioned to their dangerous scenario. Exposed publicly for lying like a rug.

Then Mrs. Harmon smiled. "Just kidding. Now what about you and the boss?"

"We're going shopping," she said. "That's all."

"For rings? Baby things? I understand you're going to Paris for a couple of weeks."

"Talk about an efficient grapevine," Derek said, coming up behind Mrs. Harmon.

She tilted her head back to watch him walk around her. "You're surprised? We sell communication stuff to NASA, remember?"

Derek frowned at his secretary with mock ferocity. "Encourage these rumors," he said, "and you'll find yourself on the next shuttle—with a one-way ticket. Anything I should know about that won't keep until Monday?"

She shook her head. "Never fear. I'm in charge."

Derek smiled at her with genuine affection. "Thank you, General Haig. See you next week."

"Aren't you going to Paris next week?" she asked sweetly as Derek and Charlotte walked away.

Derek cast her a scolding glance over his shoulder.

"ACTUALLY, IT'S NOT a bad idea when you give it some thought." Derek leaned against the glass door as Charlotte unlocked her shop. Without an assistant to help her, she'd closed the shop for the few days she was a guest of the Farnsworths.

"I am not going to Paris," Charlotte said firmly as she pushed open the door. "And that's final."

"That's narrow-minded," he corrected, following her into the cool, quiet shop. "You threw away our first honeymoon to run to Kendra's aid, and now you're throwing away our second?''

Charlotte closed and locked the door behind him and studied him in concern. "You're allowing the role to invade your reality, Derek.''

He caught her arm and pulled her closer. "*You* have invaded my reality, Charlie. I'm not sure I know up from down anymore.''

She looped an arm in his and led him companionably across a thick, rose-colored carpet. "This way is up,'' she said, pointing to an ornate oak stairway that wound upward in a graceful turn into an open gallery.

To the right of the stairs was a large open room in opulent Victorian design with an elegant settee in the middle and lace sheers and velvet drapes on the windows. At one end of the room was an out-of-character but practical three-way mirror.

On the other side of the stairs was an identical room. Behind the stairs were large double doors.

"What's back there?'' he asked.

"A veritable warehouse,'' she replied, "of classic wedding dresses, bridesmaids' gowns and suits for the men in the wedding party. I seat my clients comfortably in one of the rooms, and bring clothes out for them to make their selections.''

He smiled with new respect. "And you refer to this as a 'shop'?''

She shrugged a slender shoulder. "The word signifies elegance or chic, rather than size. Like 'boutique,' only less pretentious.'' She smiled, too. "Why? Did you imagine me slaving away in an old storefront with five dresses that I rotated over and over?''

He wasn't sure what he'd thought. But this beautiful, well-planned atmosphere wasn't it.

''No, of course not. I guess I just didn't realize the demand there must be for this sort of thing.''

''Many brides are really into outdoing each other, looking unique. Others are sincerely searching for the dress and the atmosphere that expresses the romance they feel inside. And in this day of—'' she slanted him a grin as she led him up the rose-carpeted stairs ''— speed and power, it's easier to borrow romance from another time.''

He stopped her halfway up the stairs, his eyes darkening to jet as he looked down at her.

Her eyes lightened to silver as they caught the early-afternoon glow from the leaded-glass window on the landing.

''You find yourself lacking romance?'' he asked softly.

She considered a moment as he steadied her on their precarious perch with a hand at her waist. ''Yes,'' she replied finally.

His eyebrow rose in surprise. ''After last night and this morning?''

She smiled gently, wondering if a man like him could be expected to understand the difference. ''That was passion. It's strong and deep and I doubt that anyone could be considered truly alive without knowing that aspect of life. But I'm talking about romance.''

"Isn't there romance in passion?" he asked in obvious confusion.

"Yes, but it also exists in and of itself, and that's its purest form. It's all tenderness and sweetness . . . and magic." She sighed indulgently when she saw in his eyes that he was skeptical.

She looped her arms around his neck and inclined her body against his.

"Remember this morning?" she asked.

"No," he said wryly. "My temperature goes to three hundred and six all the time. Why should I remember?"

"My point precisely." She cupped his head in her hands and brought it down to her. "I'm going to kiss you," she said, her lips so close to his they touched him as she formed her words. "And see if it doesn't haunt you with some of the same power. Maybe even more."

And then she did it—nothing more than a tender kiss, not particularly long, not particularly deep. But her hands held him with adoring tenderness, her lips, warm and dry, said a thousand silent things he hadn't heard when he'd made love to her. Her body simply leaned into his, like a flower into the wind, but he felt every gentle curve of it as though it had been a seductive caress.

He was afraid to touch her, afraid he didn't have this slow and quiet sweetness in him. He felt it to the core of his being—a slowing of the forward thrust of his life, the turbocharge that propelled his career. The power of it startled him, and he knew without a doubt that it *would* haunt him.

He drew away before she did, just a little alarmed.

Charlotte saw the concern in his eyes and felt the smallest twinge . . . like the ache of a joint that predicts a storm.

"Come on." She looped her arm in his again and tugged him the rest of the way. "You can sit on the fainting couch while I find Kendra's stockings and gloves."

"The what?"

He stopped at the top of the stairs, fascinated by the endless array of wedding paraphernalia strewn about the big, open room. In one corner of the room was a desk cluttered with papers, fabric swatches, ribbons and dried flowers.

Charlotte went to it, repeating, "Fainting couch. That thing with the elbow," as she pointed to a brocade bench sort of thing with no back and one arm that curved over at a low angle. He couldn't imagine someone being comfortable in it.

He decided to look around instead. There were tables and cases all over the room that held shoes, gloves, garters, hats, jewelry, prayer books.

Hanging on hooks were ribbons in every shade of every color. In flat boxes were lengths of lace, everything from something that looked as if it had been spun in some fairyland to big, openwork lace strewn with beads.

He stopped at a rack of formal morning coats. Above it on a shelf was a top hat. He mentally scorned its formality, then, still a little drunk on Charlotte's lesson in romance, reached for it and tried it on.

Beside it on the shelf was a walking stick with an ivory head and he took that, too. Then he went in search of a mirror.

He found a gilded oval mirror over a shelf that held several silk flower bouquets and decided that he looked stupid. He gave the hat a tilt to the side. He now looked rakish and stupid.

Behind him, Charlotte felt her heart turn to sponge. The old silk top hat had turned a very modern man into a figure from the Victorian past. He held the lazy charm of the bon vivants of the period, but in his eye, under the raffish tilt of the hat, was the danger with which he loved to flirt. Charlotte found the qualities a deadly combination.

He reached up to remove the hat, but she stopped his hand from behind. She wrapped her arms around his and leaned her chin on his shoulder to study his reflection.

Derek saw the wistful, dreamy look in her eye and felt the same stab of nerves he'd felt on the stairs. But it would take a better man than he to resist a woman who looked at him as though he was what she'd waited for a lifetime.

"What is it, madam?" he asked in an affected British accent.

"It's your hat, sir," she replied in kind, smiling at his reflection. "You look very dapper."

He tucked the walking stick under his arm. "Of course. All we lords of the manor are dapper. I've just come from winning a fortune at the tables at...oh, that gambling place. What is it called? Black's!"

He saw her blink, quirk an eyebrow, then giggle. "You mean White's?"

"Whatever." He turned to catch her in his free arm and dip her backward. "I've won Paris from the French with a straight flush and they're turning it over to me tonight at Maxim's at midnight. Are you free to join me?"

She put the back of her hand to her forehead and swooned dramatically. "Maxim's? But I've nothing to wear."

"You may borrow my hat."

She laughed throatily and he leaned down to plant a kiss at the neckline of her dress.

Her eyes darkened instantly. He swept her up in his arms and carried her to the fainting couch, overwhelmed with a need to feel her in his arms with nothing between them.

Charlotte undressed him as he undressed her, then reached her arms up for him as he put her down at the base of the couch's arm. Her feet dangled over the end.

They came together explosively, out of time with the romantic atmosphere that pervaded Borrowed Magic. They climaxed together in minutes, in direct conflict with every moody little nuance in the flowered dress on the floor on one side of the couch, and the top hat and cane on the other.

Charlotte took pleasure in their passion, and the delicious abandon she'd never known until Derek made love to her. Any concern that remained from their kiss on the stairs was lost in his arms.

Now this was a love he could relate to, Derek thought as the fire inside him subsided but continued to flame, banked but still a formidable force. Love that didn't require thought or analysis, love that didn't have to be tempered or tamed, but could be given free rein to reach as high and as deep as love could go.

He felt satisfied and faintly smug.

Then Charlotte hitched her leg up against his, lifted her head off his shoulder so that his face was shielded by a canopy of hair the color of starlight. Her silver eyes went over his face, feature by feature, with a tenderness so touching he felt it physically.

And then it began again—that invasion of weakness, the paralysis of everything that had ever meant anything to him. All that was familiar was swamped by a need to simply hold her, to touch her as though she were glass—and he was beginning to think that indeed she might be. Every time he looked into her eyes, he saw himself reflected, as someone recognizable yet unfamiliar, some alter ego.

Charlotte caught that look again and this time the little ache began to throb like real pain. She pushed off him and reached for her clothes.

He tried to catch her arm but she evaded him.

"We have to get back," she said quietly. "I still have a million details to see to.

IT WAS OBVIOUS the moment Derek and Charlotte reached the Farnsworth gate that something was wrong. It gaped open, and the limo, Caleb's Cadillac and the Morreauxs' Mercedes were parked in a line on the lane just inside.

In the middle of the narrow road, everyone in the household was gathered, all talking at once. Briane, Denise and Pauline were crying.

"My father," Charlotte said, boosting herself up in the seat as Derek drove through the gate. She scanned the little crowd and couldn't find him. Had something happened to him? Is that why everyone seemed in such a dither? "I don't see my father!"

Derek reached a hand out to push her back in her seat. "He's on the other side of the Mercedes," Derek said. "There, with Trey."

Relief flooded Charlotte as she followed Derek's pointing finger and spotted her father, obviously arguing with Trey. Everyone turned as the Porsche pulled up beside the crowd.

"What is it?" Derek asked, moving to open his car door.

Caleb pushed it closed again. "Kendra's gone," he said briefly, tightly. "I need you to go to our place in Newport Beach. The rest of us are splitting up to check the mountain cabin, the tennis club, her friend Jackie in Santa Barbara."

Off to the side of the lane, Charlotte spotted Caroline with her arm around a very tense Elizabeth.

"Oh, God," Charlotte said, letting her head fall against the back of the seat. "I knew it. She misunderstood the other night."

"No." Edward came up beside Charlotte. He placed an arm around her shoulders. "Briane says Trey suggested to Kendra this morning that they postpone the wedding for a few days while he . . . thinks things over. She saw her leave in the Corvette about ten. She thought she'd just taken a drive to cool off."

"How do you know she hasn't?" Derek asked.

"A suitcase and a few changes of clothes are missing."

Caleb handed Derek the keys. "Call when you get there. Briane and Denise will stay here to take and relay calls. If Kendra isn't there, don't rush back. Take it easy. Spend the night. I don't want you two to be highway casualties."

Derek glanced at the clock on the dash. "I'll call you the minute we arrive. An hour, an hour and a half at the most."

"Drive carefully," Edward admonished.

"I should be the one to go to Newport," Trey said, joining the little cluster. "I'm sure that's where she's gone. That's where she always goes when she has to sort things out."

He looked pale and distraught, Charlotte thought. A part of her mind not concerned with Kendra's safety wondered if he'd looked anything like this when he'd left her standing at the church a year ago.

Caleb turned on him with uncharacteristic hostility. "If it weren't for your self-involvement, she wouldn't have to sort anything out. You'll stay here! One sight of you and she'll run in the other direction."

"But I . . ."

"Leave it, Prentiss," Edward said quietly. "Trust me that it's the smartest thing to do."

Trey turned, his face purple, his jaw set, and ran to the house.

Derek spun the little car in a tight circle and headed back down the lane.

"I *knew* this was going to happen," Charlotte said, feeling responsible. "I knew I should have tried to talk to her, but I didn't know what to say. I don't lie well, even when I'm trying to do it for someone else's benefit."

"I've seen evidence of that firsthand," Derek said, braking to a stop at the road and reaching out to pat her knee comfortingly. "Don't do this to yourself. It wasn't your fault."

"I'm sure she thinks it was."

Derek turned onto the road and picked up speed. "He asked her to delay the wedding. He didn't show up for yours. How can she blame you?"

"She'll think I put him up to it. That I teased him into thinking he wanted me back."

"Is that what he told you? That he wanted you back?"

At her nod, he rolled his eyes and shook his head.

She turned in her seat to ask in mild annoyance, "You think that's unlikely? That once rid of me, a man wouldn't want me back? If so, how do you explain your own behavior?"

He smiled, unable to turn his attention from the traffic as he turned onto the main artery to the freeway.

"If I found any part of that scenario unlikely," he said, "it would be the part about letting you go in the first place. In our case, I had to let you go professionally to have any chance of reaching a personal relationship."

He sped into the traffic with impressive style and fit in neatly between a tour bus and a pickup filled with carpentry tools.

"But my reaction was for Prentiss's style." He shook his head over it once again. "We have the same problem with him at the office. When told what to do, he performs very well. When left to his own devices, he can't decide which way to move because he's basically greedy. There's no gut instinct in him that makes him do one thing or the other because it feels right. He's guided strictly by being unwilling to forfeit anything while gaining as much as he can. I don't think there's a lot of hope for him. Your father puts up with him because he was about to become Caleb's son-in-law. It was only your pleas that your father not fire him after he left you at the altar that kept him on in the first place."

"I didn't think being vengeful would help anything. He's being sent to London, isn't he?"

"The office is in good shape and it'll get him out of our hair."

Charlotte thought about Derek's assessment of Trey's character and considered it in terms of her ex-fiancé's comparison of her and Kendra.

"He said Kendra was more beautiful than I," she said, "but that she wasn't me."

This time he did glance at her, his dark eyes running quickly over her face.

He laughed pityingly. "Now I *know* there's no hope for him."

Chapter Ten

It was dusk when they reached Newport Beach, a crowded shore community fronting a harbor dotted with islands and filled with pleasure boats. Charlotte lowered her window to gulp in the clean smell of the waterfront. She hoped it might revitalize her, help her think of the right thing to say if they did find Kendra.

As Derek guided the Porsche up the road onto the dune that supported the Farnsworths' glass-walled beach house, she strained in her seat to catch a glimpse of the driveway and Kendra's white Corvette.

They rounded a bend and the driveway appeared, landscaped on both sides with potted palms and boxed geraniums. There was no car.

"Her car could be in the garage," Derek said, reading her mind.

It wasn't. Derek unlocked the back door and went through the house to the garage off the kitchen. It was full of storage boxes, neatly labeled and stacked. A bicycle stood in a corner, and a surfboard leaned against the wall. But there was no car.

"She might have stopped along the way," Derek said.

"It's only an hour and a half drive," Charlotte said, guilt and distress overtaking her. She remembered in sharp detail what it was like to be hours from your wedding—though in her case it had been minutes—and discover that you weren't loved at all, that the wonderful relationship you believed you had was a source of terror for the other person. Realizing that she generated fear in someone had required more psychological adjustment on her part than being the object of pity and embarrassment.

Then she remembered the look on Derek's face when she'd kissed him on the stairs, then on the fainting couch after they'd made love. The crisis over Kendra had put it out of her mind temporarily, but now it returned to smolder inside her. In some way she couldn't understand, her tenderness had frightened him. She was suddenly very tired of men who were afraid of love.

She went back into the kitchen and searched the cupboards for coffee. Though she'd visited the Farnsworths' Bel Air home many times, she'd never been to the beach house before.

"What are you looking for?" Derek asked, leaning a shoulder against the doorway from the garage.

"Coffee," she replied coolly, succinctly.

He crossed the kitchen and opened a long narrow cupboard in the corner that held several shelves of staples. He handed her the coffee.

She wasn't surprised that he knew his way around the house. Caleb often hosted working weekends there, or mid-crisis retreats.

"Thank you," Charlotte said politely, then concentrated on filling the pot.

"How come we're not having tea?" He could guess why, at least superficially. She was in a coffee mood suddenly, edgy, anxious and, judging by the angry little V between her eyebrows, irritable.

"We'll have to stay awake to keep track of what's happening."

He reached into the cupboard for the coffee filters and gestured as though he were handing them to her. When she reached for them, he drew them back.

"What's happening with *you?*" he asked.

She looked at him blankly. "What do you mean?" she asked and reached for the filters again. He held them out of reach.

"I mean that you've had a sudden and severe change of mood. What's wrong?"

"I'm worried about Kendra," she said impatiently. "Aren't you?"

"A little," he replied, "but I'd be more worried about her if she'd married Trey tomorrow without knowing what he's really like. My guess is, she's around somewhere. She went into town for dinner." He studied her narrowly and frowned. "I have a suspicion that your change of mood has something to do with suddenly seeing this as my fault."

She didn't hasten to deny it, but simply held her hand out for the box of filters. "I think it would be best discussed over coffee."

Trouble. He handed over the box, both intrigued and concerned.

He took down cups, she poured and they sat on a deep window seat overlooking the black night and the softly rumbling black ocean. Far in the distance were the lights of what was probably a freighter.

"What are your intentions toward me?" she asked finally, stirring nondairy creamer into her coffee.

He balanced the cup on his bent knee and blinked. "Who am I talking to? You or your father?"

"My father thinks of you as the son he never had," Charlotte replied, forcing herself to be calm and logical despite a deep need to shout and possibly throttle him. "He'd never think to ask you. I'm just looking out for myself. I've been burned once, you know."

It took him only a moment to decide he didn't like her like this. This quiet, remote individual wasn't her. He suddenly missed the romantic who always looked just a little lost, like a woman out of time and place.

"I resent being mistaken for Trey Prentiss," he said. "I thought I'd made it clear I was nothing like him."

"You aren't," she agreed, taking a sip of coffee. She swallowed and leaned her head back against the deep window frame. "At least not visibly. But you do share something with him, don't you?"

"A company car on occasion."

She ignored his attempt at humor and said, "I'm talking about your assessment of him earlier today.

You said he couldn't make decisions because he didn't want to forfeit anything while gaining everything he wanted.''

He waited for her to explain. He recalled the remark, but he couldn't connect it with himself.

"When I kissed you on the stairs in my shop," she explained quietly, turning her head to look out the window as though she didn't want to look at him, "I frightened you."

"Charlie . . ."

"Don't try to deny it, Derek," she admonished quietly, finally leveling her gaze on him. It was grave and sad. "I know what fear looks like. I frightened Trey, too."

Derek put his cup down in a space between the cushions. It gave him time to think. He wouldn't lie, but he also couldn't explain to her what he didn't understand himself.

"Any man," he said candidly, "who denies feeling fear in the face of a relationship that addles his brain and weakens his defenses is a liar. And it isn't fear of you, it's fear of . . . love, I guess. Fear of not having that sweet stuff you seem to need."

She held his gaze and he saw a small glimmer of respect in her eyes. Then she lowered them, still cool, still remote.

She raised them again, and fixed him with what felt like a laser gaze. He knew he was in trouble.

"Then what is it you feel when we're in bed?" she asked conversationally. "You certainly show no fear there. What am I at that moment, if I'm not an addler of your brain or a threat to your defenses? A distraction? A toy? Just a little R and R for the brilliant young executive?''

Anger began to simmer inside him. ''Have you ever felt like a toy in my arms?''

Their gazes locked. She finally put her cup down and folded her arms. ''No, I haven't. But then I've discovered you're the consummate actor. You're never at a loss for the right move or the right line. I suppose this is all my fault for taking on my role too completely.''

''What 'this' are you talking about?'' he demanded. ''To the best of my recollection, nothing has changed since we made love this afternoon, and you certainly didn't seem to feel as though you were being treated like anything less than the woman I love.''

''I saw that look in your eyes again. Like when I kissed you on the stairs.''

''Good God!'' Derek sprang to his feet, what remained of his patience evaporating. ''It seems to me you're missing an important point. If you're intent on comparing me with Trey, you might notice that I'm still around.''

He'd expected that to bring her up short, to make her look sheepish. When she held his gaze evenly, he began to wonder if they were speaking the same language.

''And what happens tomorrow, after the wedding? If there is a wedding.''

''What do you mean?''

"You've said nothing about continuing our relationship or about making it permanent. I think you're more afraid than you realize."

Derek jammed his hands into his pockets and stalked away from her half the width of the room, then stalked back. He stopped in front of her and freed one hand to make a "There! See!" gesture.

"This is precisely why you don't belong in business, or maybe even in life. You assemble all available data and come to a completely erroneous conclusion."

She looked implacably into the temper in his eyes. "Then you were going to propose?"

"No, I wasn't," he replied brutally, "because the kind of mess you had with Trey, and the kind of mess he and Kendra are now having, is what results when you try to write a contract around something as nebulous as feelings!"

"Really?" She didn't change expression. "Curious that it's worked for several thousand years."

"No, it hasn't. The wedding contract is a relatively new refinement. And you call this working? A 50 percent divorce rate?"

"Marriages work beautifully when people believe in them!" she said, standing, too. She was beginning to lose her grip on control.

"In the last century, when people followed tradition without question. And that's the age you prefer—" he pointed a finger at her shoulder "—because it was a sweet, amenable time. Well, this isn't! We're a society more aware of our options. And it's simply foolish to write a contract around love. It isn't bankable."

"Bankable?" she shrieked, unable to believe he'd used the word. "Bankable!" she repeated it to assure herself she'd heard it. "God, if that isn't the Cabot party line. If you can't put it in the bank and draw interest on it, it isn't worth having. Well, let me tell you something."

She went to him, stopping within inches of his chest and straining pugnaciously up at him. "Here's a basic truth you've apparently never figured out. There are valuable things in life that *cost you.*" She emphasized the last two words and spoke them slowly. "I know that's an alien concept for you, but it's true. They will never make you a calculable profit, because if you're lucky enough to acquire them, you have to give as much as you get. That may not be sound business, but it's life!

"And one more thing." She'd lowered her voice and, furious as he was, he found himself hanging on her every word. She was fascinating in a rage.

"Men and women of the last century were as aware of their options as we are. They just never considered cowardice one."

She stormed away, leaving him alone in the middle of the dark living room.

"SHE WASN'T at the cabin or the club," Briane reported when Derek called the Farnsworth home. "We haven't heard from Santa Barbara yet. If she's not in Newport, that's our last hope."

"We're hoping she just went out to dinner or something, and will be back," he said bracingly. He wasn't sure he believed it. In fact, he was convinced if Kendra were smart she was on a 747 right now getting as far away from Prentiss and her mother as she could.

"We'll call you if we hear anything," Briane said. "Thanks, Derek."

"Sure. I'll be in touch."

"Any news?"

Derek looked up in surprise as he cradled the receiver. He hadn't seen hide nor hair of Charlotte in the hour since their altercation. He'd heard a door slam somewhere upstairs and thought it better not to investigate.

"No sign of her so far," he said. "But they haven't heard from Santa Barbara yet."

Charlotte stood on tiptoe to look into the freezer part of the refrigerator. She had shed her shoes, and her face had a red and puffy look, as though she'd slept— or cried.

"I've got a couple of frozen quiches in the oven," Derek said.

Charlotte closed the freezer door and turned to look at the stove for confirmation. There were twelve minutes left on the oven timer.

"Two for you," she asked wryly, looking through the cupboards, "or is one of them mine? I thought I saw a can of asparagus in here."

"They're both *yours*," he said, moving to reach into a high cupboard over the stove. "You're the one who wants everything. Voilà." He handed her the asparagus.

"I don't want everything," she said reasonably. She'd come downstairs determined not to argue with him. She didn't want to upset what would probably be their last few hours together with anger and recrimination. "I just can't see myself in a prolonged affair. But let's not fight about it. I'm going to magnanimously allow you one of the quiches, and half of the asparagus."

"Thank you."

"Don't mention it."

"Charlie, this is nuts," he said, turning her away from the can opener and into his arms. "You're imagining a problem that isn't there. We've had a wonderful few days. The rest of our lives could be as wonderful."

She gently but firmly pushed his arms from around her. "Not when I know you don't consider my feelings for you . . . bankable."

"Maybe I don't doubt you. Maybe I doubt me."

That seemed to shake her. She said gravely, "Then that's even worse."

"God, that's not what I meant!" he said, feeling like a man on the edge of a limb he was sawing off himself. "I meant that I've always moved too fast to slow down and think about things. It's not that my love for you isn't genuine and deep. It's that I can't imagine signing my name to a contract that's about what I feel. I've been in business long enough to know that even the most reliable numbers can turn on you."

She pushed him gently into a chair. "Then you have to do what you have to do. And so do I. Unfortunately that isn't going to be the same—'' she swallowed and finished a little shakily ''—the same thing.'' Then she drew a breath and went back to the asparagus.

He set the table while she served, and they sat at opposite sides of a small kitchen table and looked out at the darkness. They were silent, except to ask for the salt or the butter.

After they'd finished, Derek excused himself to take a shower. He desperately needed something to assuage his confusion and frustration. Had he made love to this woman only hours ago on a fainting couch in a Victorian loft caught on a time snag?

Charlotte made another pot of coffee, then straightened up the kitchen. She wandered out to the glass wall in the living room that looked out on the ocean and stared without seeing.

That had been close, she thought, trying to feel philosophical rather than sad. She'd almost found the right man, even though all indicators showed him to be the wrong one. He wasn't laid-back or romantic, but he made her feel very special, very right.

They could have coped with their different approaches to life, she was sure, if only he hadn't been frightened by the prospect. Well. She shook her head at her reflection. If she ever got interested in another man, she'd just have to learn to be less scary.

She reached over to turn off the light on the side table and, sliding the window aside, stepped out onto the patio. A brisk breeze blew filled with the fragrance of fall. A little chill rippled up her arms and she crossed them, tossing her hair back and out of her face.

And that was when she saw her. Moonlight shone in a bright wedge that started some distance offshore. Trapped in it, bobbing like a piece of flotsam, was a bright blond head.

"Kendra," she whispered to herself, then certain the figure was the missing bride, probably bent on self-destruction, she shouted as she ran to the door, "Derek!" she shouted. "Kendra's in the water! Derek!"

Charlotte slipped and slid down the rocky trail to the sand. Then she ran for all she was worth, still shouting Kendra's name. The sand slowed her progress, and now on a level with the water, she'd lost sight of the figure in it.

Finally at the water's edge, she kicked off her shoes and ran into the surf. It was shockingly cold. She dove forward, lost her breath in a gasp, then swallowed a mouthful of water.

She swam powerfully but awkwardly, fear making her strokes uneven. If Kendra succeeded in killing herself, she, Charlotte, would kill Trey personally—slowly.

"Kendra!" she shouted again. "Kendra!"

A fair distance out, she stopped to tread water, hoping to spot Kendra somewhere ahead of her. But she saw nothing. A cloud had slid over the moon, and her eyes caught nothing in the direction of the ocean but absolute blackness. She turned in a circle, panic making her already labored breathing come even harder.

"Oh, Kendra," she groaned.

Behind her she saw Derek run into the water and start toward her with firm, even strokes. She started forward again, unwilling to believe Kendra had accomplished her task.

Then something rose out of the water just ahead of her. She screamed as water spewed like a fountain, then rained down on her. Images of Bitsy Tate's column carrying her gleeful obituary passed before her eyes—Once-dumped Society Woman Serves As Payback For The Sushi Craze As Shark Eats Her Raw.

"*What* are you shouting about," Kendra demanded, "and *what* are you doing here?"

Charlotte discovered that surprise was buoyant. She bobbed in the water as she stared at the shadowy features of the young woman who'd become her friend in the days they'd worked together.

Kendra appeared to be fine. Water spiked her eyelashes and made her wet hair lay back against her scalp. The moon reappeared, highlighting her beautiful bone structure.

"I thought you were..." Charlotte, now feeling foolish, pointed out to sea. "I mean, it looked as though you might be..."

Kendra frowned, then rolled her eyes as she realized what Charlotte couldn't say. "Oh, Charlie," she scolded. "I'm mad as hell, but I am not suicidal."

Charlotte sagged with relief and swallowed another mouthful of water. Kendra held her up.

"Your parents were frantic," Charlotte said sharply. "Briane saw you tear off in the Corvette after you argued with Trey, and everyone at the house split up to try to find you. Your father sent Derek and me here."

Derek reached them, spraying them with water again as he splashed to a stop beside them. "Are you all right?" he demanded of Kendra.

"Fine," she assured him, wiping water from her face. "I just needed to get away from everyone and decide what to do. I'm amazed that didn't occur to anyone."

"You were gone a long time," Charlotte said righteously. "And the circumstances made everyone presume the worst."

"Let's talk about this on solid ground," Derek said. He pushed them gently ahead of him toward shore.

"YOU SHOULD HAVE left a note, or called when you got here." Charlotte wasn't sure why, but she'd appointed herself maiden aunt in charge of scolding.

They all sat around the Swedish fireplace in the living room, wrapped in thick robes and sipping cognac. The furniture was low, the decor white and stark. Charlotte couldn't dispel the feeling that she was in an alien environment.

"I was too angry to leave a note," Kendra said calmly, "and I didn't get here until fifteen or twenty minutes ago."

Derek frowned. "Where's your car?"

"Ran out of gas," she confessed in self-deprecation. "I didn't even check the tank when I left the house, and I drove all over the place, trying to cool off. I stopped for a cappuccino in town and sat on the sand for a long time. Then I headed here and ran out of gas about a quarter of a mile down the beach.''

She downed the last of her brandy and put her snifter aside, looking suddenly tired and a little shaken. "I walked here . . .''

"In the dark?" Charlotte asked with disapproval.

Kendra ignored her and went on. "And all I wanted to do before I came inside was go for a swim. I thought it might loosen me up, clear my head..." She drew her knees up and rested her chin on them. Her voice became unsteady. "Make me believe it was all a bad dream.''

Charlotte, sitting beside her on the floor, reached out to put an arm around her. "I'm sorry," she said. "Contrary to how this platitude usually sounds, I know just how you feel.''

Kendra sniffed and raised her head to give Charlotte a grim smile. "You know, I remember how you looked that day when you came into the church to tell us that Trey wasn't coming. At first I thought you were silly to have done it. I know your father would have if you'd asked him. Or Caroline. Now I know how brave you were. And maybe even why you did it. You had to prove to yourself that you had guts even if he hadn't any.''

"What are you going to do?" Derek asked.

"I don't know." Kendra wrapped her arms around her legs and looked into the fire, her face flushed, her eyes unfocused.

"I've been thinking about going to Europe.''

Charlotte sighed. "I'd love to have time for that. I think you should go for it."

"I've always thought I'd pursue my painting one day, but I've never mustered the ambition. Maybe now I'll do it."

She dropped her knees to sit Indian-style and continued to stare at the fire. "I'll live in a garret like the romantic image...." She turned to smile wanly at Derek, then at Charlotte. "But my monthly allowance will save me from romantic starvation." Her smile crumpled almost immediately and she began to cry. "I love him—the jerk!"

Charlotte helped her up to bed.

"I know you don't believe this now," she said, helping her turn down the bed, "but you'll get over him."

Kendra nodded, still crying quietly. "I think the problem is, he never got over *you.*"

Charlotte straightened, coming around the bed to push Kendra into a sitting position and sit beside her.

"This has nothing to do with me," she said firmly. "He loves being in love, but he's afraid of promising anything more, so he keeps backing out. In this case, he had to find a convenient excuse to do it."

Kendra looked at her evenly. "He did try to come on to you that night in my father's study, didn't he?"

Charlotte nodded. "But it isn't because he loves me. It was because he was unconsciously setting himself up to let you down."

Kendra kicked a foot out angrily.

"I ought to drug him and drag him through the ceremony, anyway, and then make his life as miserable as he seems to think I would."

Charlotte laughed softly. "That does have a certain appeal. I think it's illegal, though. Europe sounds like a much more positive solution to me. Why don't you get some sleep? We'll have to be up early in the morning."

"I know," she said. She looked at Charlotte, her eyes miserable. "I hope I can be as composed as you were."

"The minute I was finished," Charlotte said, "I drove home and threw everything glass in the house into the fireplace. It was very satisfying."

Kendra climbed under the blanket and Charlotte pulled it up over her, then turned off the light.

Charlotte stopped at the door and turned to the figure now huddled in the fetal position under the blue-and-white quilt. "Try to think of it as a fresh start. As the first day of your career as an artist."

"Yeah," Kendra said, her voice containing little enthusiasm. "Right. Good night, Charlie."

Charlotte went back downstairs to clean up the kitchen and found that Derek had already done it.

"How is she?" he asked. He had changed out of the robe into jeans and a white T-shirt. He sat on the window seat in the living room, one knee drawn up, the other foot braced on the carpet while he sipped another cognac. The room was lit only by the glow from the fireplace.

Charlotte stopped halfway into the room, afraid to go any farther. She felt the pull of his attraction for her, the draw of his touch, and knew it was smarter to keep her distance.

"Tired, sad. But I'm sure she'll recover."

Derek felt the gap between them, and knew it was wider than the space that physically separated them. Annoyed that she could be cool when he felt like raging, he said, "It wasn't very smart of you to run into the water in the dark."

That would ignite a reaction, he was sure.

She looked back at him for several seconds, her slender body lost in the voluminous folds of the robe. But there'd never been anything slender about her dignity. The duchess was back.

"I considered waiting for daylight," she replied calmly, "but I wasn't sure she could hold her breath for seven and a half hours."

Temper erupted in him, hot and quick. He swung his legs off the window seat and stood. "You had shouted for me. You could have waited two minutes!"

"If she *had* been drowning," Charlotte said, gripping control with both hands, "she could have been dead in two minutes!"

"And so could you! That would have helped her a lot!"

"It would have helped you!" she shouted at him. "My life insurance is more 'bankable' than my love. And you've got everyone convinced you're my husband. You might have been able to collect."

He grabbed the lapels of her robe before he could think twice about it and yanked her toward him.

Charlotte saw the fury in his eyes and couldn't begin to guess what would happen next. There was violence in his eyes and in his grip.

Only conditioning by a father who'd taught him to respect women, and a personal code that prevented him from hurting anyone or anything that wasn't at least as strong as he, prevented him from giving her the swat that remark deserved.

Still, he couldn't deny that he enjoyed the trepidation in her eyes just a little bit.

"You're going to pay for that, Charlotte," he said with quiet menace as he reached inside her robe.

Her hands closed on his forearms, but she couldn't stop him from cupping one hand on her hip and splaying the other against her back.

"Derek Cabot, if you dare..." she began to threaten.

"Charlie, shut up," he said, and held her immobile against him while he leaned over and kissed her. It occurred to him that he was punishing himself far more than he was hurting her, but he was driven to do it all the same.

She wriggled and struggled, and the intimate contact seemed to rob the anger from him and turn it into longing. The longing gentled his touch—and gentled her.

Then her arms were wrapped around his neck and she was kissing him as though the great gap had never opened between them. It was two days ago in the bathtub, this afternoon in the Victorian loft.

The phone rang, loud and shrilly. Derek didn't hear it for a moment, then it rang again and he felt Charlotte pushing at him.

He knew the moment he raised his head that the interruption had brought her quickly back to awareness. Her lavender-gray eyes accused him of more things than he could decipher at a glance.

The phone rang again, and he thought wryly that it was like a safety signal. Great yawning cavity, it said. Don't fall in.

Keeping a hold on Charlotte's hand, he pulled her with him into the kitchen to the wall phone. She slapped at his arm and pried at his fingers, but he held on.

It was Trey.

"I want to speak to Kendra," he said urgently.

Added to Trey's already long list of sins, destroying that fragile moment with Charlotte was going to get him murdered.

"Kendra is asleep," Derek said in a forbidding tone.

"I don't believe it," Trey said after a moment. "She just spoke to her father half an hour ago."

"That was half an hour ago," Derek replied with sorely strained patience. "Now she's asleep."

"I have to talk to her."

"It'll wait until morning."

"I have to talk to her *now.*"

Derek held the phone to his chest and consulted Charlotte, who had stopped struggling.

"It's Trey," he said quietly. "He wants to talk to Kendra. He says it can't wait until morning."

She snatched the phone from him. "She's asleep after almost drowning, thanks to you!" She avoided Derek's gaze when his dark eyebrow rose to note the fib. "If you call here again before morning we won't even bring her home. We'll take her straight to the airport."

"The airport? No! Charlie, wait! I..."

She slammed the receiver with relish. Then yanked out of Derek's grip. She gave him a thoughtful, strangely satisfied little smile. "I might even join her. Good night, Cabot. Sleep tight."

Chapter Eleven

The florist was draping the iron gate with a garland of white roses interspersed with baby's breath when Derek turned the Porsche onto the Farnsworth estate.

They were halfway up the lane when everyone streamed from the house to greet them, Bitsy in the spearhead, Darby already snapping photographs.

"I'll take you around the back," Derek said, "and we'll go in through the garages."

"No, it's all right." Kendra smoothed her hair back and drew a deep breath. In the only slightly mussy white cotton pants and shirt she'd worn the day before, she appeared remarkably serene. Her hair was caught back in a loose knot, and she appeared to be precisely what she was—the product of a long line of blue blood.

"What did you tell yourself," she asked Charlotte when Derek was forced to slow the car as the Farnsworth household swarmed around it, "when you faced the church filled with people."

"That the problem was Trey's and not mine," she replied. "I was just the one who had to deal with it."

"That's good." Kendra patted her hand, then opened the car door.

Darby's camera clicked as Elizabeth enfolded Kendra in her arms, her aquiline profile marred just for an instant with a rush of emotion. Then Elizabeth pulled herself together and held Kendra at arm's length.

"Are you all right?" she demanded quietly.

"I'm fine," Kendra replied.

Caleb came forward to take her into his arms. "Ah, Kennie," he said gruffly. "We were so worried about you."

"I'm fine, Daddy." She kissed his cheek. "I needed a little time alone to decide what to do."

"Kendra. Kendra!" Trey broke through the little crowd, fighting off Babs's grip as she tried to pull him back. "Kendra, please."

He broke free of Babs, then had to contend with Caleb, who turned to block Trey's path to his daughter.

"Daddy, it's all right," Kendra said, gently pushing her father aside and confronting Trey with a look so dispassionate Charlotte had to admire it. "What is it, Trey? I thought you were going away."

Charlotte saw the lost look in his eyes. The Kendra who'd come home was not the Kendra he knew.

"I'd like to talk to you," he said, glancing furtively at the group gathered around them. "Somewhere where we can be alone for a few minutes."

"Of course," she said. But there was condescension in her tone, not cooperation.

Bitsy, who had apparently missed the subtlety, asked, "Then the wedding's on?"

Kendra smiled her way as the crowd opened a path for her. "No, it's not. I'm leaving for Europe on an evening flight."

Trey, who'd fallen into step behind her, stopped in his tracks. She took a step back to hook her arm in his and pull him along. "Come on. We'll take a walk."

Bitsy came to stand beside Charlotte as everyone watched Trey and Kendra walk away.

"She wouldn't!" Elizabeth said on a low gasp, then turned to Caleb with a look of horror. "I finally have Trey talked around and she says she's going to Europe?"

Caleb studied her mutely for a moment, then asked quietly, "You did what?"

But the rest of their conversation was lost when Bitsy elbowed Charlotte. "Want to tell me what happened?"

Charlotte felt unutterably weary suddenly and wanted nothing more than to sit in the guest house living room with a cup of tea and go over the next months' schedule in her day timer.

"You'll have to ask Kendra that," she replied.

"She's planning to go to Europe?"

"Could be."

"But Trey's changed his mind."

"No news there, Bitsy. Trey's always changing his mind."

Edward and Caroline joined them, Edward putting his arm around Charlotte and kissing her temple.

"How are you, sweets? I thought you sounded a little grim last night on the phone."

Grim? Yes. That was a good word. She forced a smile for him. "I know what Kendra's going through. I wish I could do more for her."

Caroline linked her arm in Derek's and smiled up at him with sympathy. "And how are you holding up in the midst of all this chaos? This isn't comfortable ground for a man who likes order and efficiency."

He shrugged negligently, glancing at Charlotte with turbulent brown eyes. "Charlie's converting me."

Caroline studied the look that passed between Derek and her stepdaughter, then met her husband's quick surreptitious glance with one of concern.

"You know..." Bitsy said. Everyone turned to look at her, surprised she was still there. "If you two can't answer my questions about Kendra, maybe there's something else you can tell me."

Charlotte felt danger in her bones. Here it comes, she told herself, feeling the finger of trepidation hit every vertebra from the base of her skull to the small of her back.

Derek's arm came around her, surprisingly comfortable under the circumstances.

"What is it?" he asked affably.

"You said you were married during a recent business trip."

Charlotte felt that strum up her spinal column one more time.

"That's right," Derek replied.

Bitsy uttered a little laugh of confusion. In truth, she didn't look confused at all. She looked curiously pleased. "Well, I don't understand. I know you spent two days in San Francisco two weeks ago, and a weekend in Denver last week."

"Yes."

"Well..." That little laugh again. "It's the most curious thing. I can't find a health certificate or a marriage license registered in either county. How do you explain that?"

By telling you we're frauds, Charlotte replied to herself in a sort of repressed panic. *By admitting that Caroline, with all good intentions, placed us in this impossible position where we could do nothing but lie and deceive and humiliate everyone involved.*

She felt an hysterical giggle try to rise in her throat. She cleared it and folded her arms in an attempt to stave it off.

Unfortunately for me, I've fallen victim to my own best performance. I'm in love with this man who rushed to my rescue, then panicked when I turned into his arms. There's an interesting parallel between Trey and Kendra and Derek and me if you were...

Charlotte's thoughts and the reply Derek had begun were interrupted by Caleb's booming voice.

"Good God, woman! I know you're expecting hundreds of people in just four hours, but the girl's had a traumatic experience. For once in your life, think about something besides yourself and how *you* will look. If she takes him back, I would say she needs psychiatric counseling, but we will have a wedding. If she doesn't, we'll send her with Henry to the airport and host a party to celebrate her good sense.''

"Caleb Farnsworth!'' Elizabeth gasped, her cheeks Chianti red. ''What do you think ... ?''

''I'll tell you what I think!'' he said, taking hold of her elbow and pulling her with him toward the house. ''I've been itching to tell you what's been on my mind for thirty years. You're going to hear it now, Elizabeth—at high volume!''

Everyone watched in amazement as the usually gentle giant turned hostile husband and marched Elizabeth into the house. As the Morreauxs and Derek exchanged amused glances, Bitsy turned from the scene to smile broadly.

''God. This is turning into the story of a lifetime.''

Caroline returned her smile with one filled with sarcasm. ''I'm happy for you. Excuse us.''

''Just a minute.'' Bitsy caught Derek's arm to stop him from following Edward and Caroline. ''You haven't answered my question.''

Oh, God. Charlotte had thought for a moment there they were going to escape. The arm Derek had around her tightened as he felt her fidget.

''You didn't find a health certificate or a wedding license in Denver or San Francisco,'' he said, ''because we were married in Massachusetts.''

She frowned. ''That wasn't on your schedule.''

''It came up suddenly.'' He squeezed Charlotte to him. ''We took advantage of it. Excuse us. We haven't had much sleep, and whatever happens this afternoon I'd like to be awake for it.''

Derek led Charlotte to the path to the guest house and beckoned to her parents to follow. They clustered in the small living room, looking at one another in concern.

"She knows," Charlotte said, pacing a small path from the mirrored wall to the door. "I know she knows."

"She's not sure of anything," Derek said. "She'd like us to be lying, but she's not sure."

Charlotte stopped to look at him, a frail hope in her eyes. "Did you really go to Massachusetts in the past two weeks?"

He shook his head, grinning. He leaned an elbow against the high back of Caroline's chair. "No. But I wasn't specific about where we were married. She'll have to check every county before she knows for certain. By then this will all be over, one way or another."

Edward nodded from a corner of the sofa. "The important thing is not to panic. Caleb's been through a lot in the past two days. He doesn't need further embarrassment."

"So, please don't let down now, darling," Caroline said from the chair opposite the sofa. "Keep up the pretense a little while longer, then you may berate me all you like when the wedding's over—or whatever happens."

Charlotte sank onto the sofa and let her head fall against the back. It was only ten in the morning, but she felt as though she could sleep for days. Lying was so exhausting.

She heard the silence pulse for several seconds, then her father's rumbling voice asked, "Unless pretending will be more of a problem today than it's been the past few days. You two have . . . a spat?"

Charlotte didn't even open her eyes. She didn't want to see the look in Derek's. A spat, indeed. "How do you do that?" she asked her father.

"I can read you like an annual report," Edward replied. "And Derek and I have a kind of mind link that happens to people who work closely for a long time. I know something's suddenly wrong between you."

Charlotte opened her eyes then to look at her father. He was so sharp, so cool. She gave a moment's serious thought to asking Derek and Caroline to leave, then climbing into her father's lap and telling him everything.

But she'd coped a year ago; she could cope today.

She made herself look at Derek. He seemed to have slipped into the mood he'd been in the morning she'd awakened him with kisses when Elizabeth and Bitsy had been at the door. His dark eyes were calm and remote.

"I can act like a devoted wife," she said, wanting to shake him out of that calm. "I was getting so into it, I almost believed it myself."

Derek heard the jibe and took it without complaint. He wasn't going to get into a battle of witty double entendres. His wit had fled, and he suddenly didn't understand anything.

"Piece of cake," he said.

Edward looked from one to the other. Caroline drew in a breath to ask a question and he silenced her with a look. Then he stood and helped her to her feet.

"As long as no one does anything radical out of a misguided sense of conscience or... anything else."

"I'm never radical," Derek assured him.

He gave him a masculine glance. "It's not you I'm worried about. Come along, Caro."

"But, Edward, I..." She gestured toward the sofa where Charlotte still sat in a disconsolate slump.

He tugged her relentlessly toward the door. "It isn't your business, my love. See you two later."

"She's been my business since the day I married you," she insisted mildly as he pushed her before him through the open door.

"You've passed the torch, Caroline."

"I have? I don't remember pa—"

Their voices trailed away as the door closed behind them. Derek locked it.

"Want a cup of tea?" he asked, heading for the kitchen.

"I'd kill for a cup of tea," Charlotte replied wearily.

He didn't even smile. "I know you'd love the opportunity to do murder, but it isn't necessary. I'll bring it."

Charlotte closed her eyes and listened to the very domestic sounds of him puttering around the kitchen. Unbidden, memories of their argument of the night before played over in her mind.

She cringed a little at her vitriolic turn of mood when they discovered Kendra wasn't at the house. Why had she turned on him like that? Certainly there was a difference between a man who admitted to feeling fear, and another who acted on it.

That kind of angry judgment was unlike her. Though Trey had hurt and humiliated her, she'd been able to be civil to him and chalk it all up to experience.

Derek she had flayed with condemnation.

She heard the kettle whistle and sat up and smoothed her hair. There was still a serious problem here, but an apology on her part was definitely in order.

Derek walked in with the cup, placed it in front of her without the twitch of a muscle in his face.

"If you're comfortable there," he said, "I'm going to sack out on the bed for an hour or so."

"Derek, I…" He straightened and met her gaze, his eyes completely blank of feeling of any kind. It occurred to her that she'd killed it. Misery as well as guilt settled in her stomach like bad doughnuts. He would probably not even hear an apology at the moment, much less accept one. "Sure," she said. "Go ahead. Thanks for the tea."

He closed the bedroom door quietly behind him. She sipped the steaming brew, a salty, solitary tear falling into it.

A SENSE OF WAITING pervaded everything. The broad back lawn that had teemed with activity while tents were set up, tables and chairs brought in, garden gate-like trellises arranged to give the vastness a definition, was now quiet. People still worked, because no one was certain yet of the ultimate outcome, but the cheer a festive wedding brought was gone.

Stepping out onto the guest house's little porch with her tea, Charlotte spotted Briane and Denise wandering among the workers, their extravagant good looks making them look like actresses hired for a play that had been canceled.

She hurried out to intercept them.

"Any news?" she asked.

Briane shook her head. "They're still talking."

Denise smiled wryly and pointed to one of the workers. He was particularly tall with well-defined pecs and slightly long dark hair. "If Kendra does call the whole thing off," she said, "I'm considering marrying him just so all this isn't wasted."

Charlotte walked with them across the rich green turf. It took an army of gardeners, she knew, to keep the grass this lush and green in the semitropical southern California climate.

Briane sighed. "I know it would be embarrassing for the family, but I hope she does go to Europe."

"She claims to still love Trey," Charlotte said.

Briane stepped into one of the garden arches and pulled the other two in after her, as though believing the wide openwork would afford them privacy.

"I would never tell her this," she said, her green eyes distressed. Her glance darted to Denise, whom she obviously had told. Denise shook her head in disgust. "But I overheard Mrs. Farnsworth talking to Trey late yesterday afternoon."

The warm morning air was still as Charlotte waited, a sense of foreboding taking over her already troubled spirit.

"Trey changed his mind because she offered him money. Big money."

"But he has money," Charlotte said.

"I'm talking high seven figures that he wouldn't have to share with four other siblings."

Charlotte digested that information while trying to decide what to do. Elizabeth had literally bought Trey for Kendra. Every instinct insisted that Kendra should know that.

"I think Briane should tell her," Denise said quietly, "but she's afraid whatever Kendra decides it would only hurt her more. Imagine your mother choosing to buy a man who no longer wants you, rather than suffer a few hours embarrassment."

Charlotte smiled thinly as she thought of Caroline, who'd had to be refrained from hiring a hit man for Trey when he'd done this same thing to Charlotte.

"No, I can't. Well. We'll just have to wait and see what she decides to do."

"Right."

Briane placed an arm around Charlotte and squeezed her shoulders. "See how lucky you were to have escaped Trey Prentiss and found your gorgeous husband?"

It wasn't difficult to dredge up a smile. Gallows humor could be powerful stuff.

"Wasn't I? I'd better get back to him. If you hear anything, let me know."

"I will." Briane looked at her watch and frowned. "It's already after eleven."

Denise added unnecessarily, "The invitations say two."

Charlotte walked back to the guest house with determination in her step. If Derek was sleeping, she intended to wake him up. She had to know how he truly felt. And she had to tell him how she felt—that she loved him more than anything.

As that thought formed in her mind, she was reminded of two days earlier when they'd first admitted love to each other. She remembered telling him angrily that she didn't intend to surrender to it. She realized now that she'd felt that way because *she'd* been afraid.

Was this the famous transference psychologists talked about, attributing your own unsatisfactory qualities to someone else?

She burst through the front door, marched across the living room and into the bedroom—to find it empty, the bed made. She went to the closet.

Loss overwhelmed her as her eyes fell on her own things—skirts, slacks, sweaters. His sport coats were gone, the colorful array of sweaters on the shelf. His shaving bag was gone from the bathroom.

She ran for the door, intent on finding him before he got away. She hadn't been gone that long and he wouldn't leave without speaking to his host and hostess, without talking to her father. She told herself bracingly that if she hurried, she could intercept him at the garages.

She tore the door open.

"Hi." Kendra stood there, still in her whites. The knot at the back of her hair was disheveled, and it looked as though her composure was, too. "Do you have time . . . to talk?" she asked.

No! she wanted to scream. *I don't have time. For the first time in my life I want to hurry before Derek gets away!*

But she knew the look on Kendra's face. She'd worn it herself a year ago—a hurt so deep, a self-esteem so low, logical thought simply could not function. The anguish had to be poured out to someone. Caroline had listened to her for hours.

"Of course," she said, drawing Kendra inside.

In her mind's eye, she saw Henry hand over the keys to the Porsche, saw Derek climb into it without opening the door, back unerringly out of the garage, give Henry a wave and turn in a tight circle, then drive away.

DEREK WAS LOOKING for anyone he recognized, but all he encountered were the florist's staff, the caterers, the men from the rental company that was providing the tents, the tables and chairs. He'd tried every room downstairs including Caleb's study, and now peered around a corner of the kitchen that was filled with the caterers' crew.

Then he saw Babs, sitting at the butcher-block table in the corner, sipping moodily at a jigger of something clear. She spotted him and beckoned him over.

"Cabot," she said, her eyes perfectly sober, though sad. "How are ya? Ever get that pretty girl to remember she was married to you?"

He slipped into the captain's chair opposite her. "Only once in a while. She has a selective memory."

She nodded. "Don't we all." She pointed in the direction of the caterers arranging food on trays, sliding pans into the oven, scurrying back and forth across the large room. "There was a time when all the women in the family got together to do this for the bride. Not strangers that had to be paid."

Derek nodded. He remembered his cousin's wedding. His mother had baked for days, and she and his aunts had met every afternoon for weeks to make her a quilt. But he had other things on his mind at the moment to spare too much emotion for the sad loss of the... His mind groped for the word. Resisted the one that came to mind. Groped again, then finally had to surrender and settle for the only one that properly applied. Without Charlotte, he felt a sad loss of the *romance* of things.

He suddenly realized that Babs's problems and his own might be more allied than he'd thought.

"I'm looking for Caleb," he said. "Do you know where he is? Or Edward?"

She took another small sip from her jigger. She held it up to him. "Want me to pour you one? Best medicine God ever made."

Derek shook his head. "Thanks."

Babs pointed her index finger to the ceiling. "Caleb and Elizabeth are screaming at each other in their bedroom, and I think your father-in-law is on a long-distance call. He walked outside with the portable phone."

Derek frowned and made himself relax in his chair. It didn't sound as though either man could be interrupted at the moment. He'd intended to thank Caleb for his hospitality, try to explain briefly to Edward what had gone on between him and his daughter and assure him that he hadn't hurt her deliberately, that the brief amity they'd achieved was over and the best thing he could do for both of them was take off the moment the wedding was over—or Kendra left for the airport, whichever resulted. Maybe he could be transferred back to New York. Maybe he could give Kendra and Charlotte the two tickets to Paris.

"You look like you've been hit in the stomach with a brick," Babs diagnosed. "Having more trouble with Charlotte than her remembering your name?"

He looked into the bright, wise eyes and found it easy to be honest. "Yes. Sometimes the way she makes me feel frightens me because...it's so different from anything I've ever felt before. And *that* frightens her. She thinks it means I'm like Prentiss. That I'd walk away from her one day."

"But you married her," she said frowning. "You promised to stay with her. Doesn't that tell her something?"

That was as far as he could go. He wished now he'd said yes to the drink. "Guess not," he said.

Babs shook her head over the state of modern marriages. "I think the trouble is, your generation got so into thinking about yourselves. That's good in a way. Supposed to cause less guilt, less anger. But it takes away the need to share."

She smiled thoughtfully, memories traveling through her unfocused gaze. "Elizabeth's father and I raised sheep. Rough life. Hard work. Lizzy doesn't like to remember that. Thinks it's dirty somehow. But it was more real than this. We loved each other, leaned on each other, took from each other and gave each other everything we had."

She touched the bowl that sat before her on the table, the one that contained the sourdough starter she'd brought all the way from Montana, and that would *not* be used for the wedding.

"It's like this starter. You add and you take away and it goes on forever." She folded her arms and smiled across the table at him. "With the new ideas about separate but equal, and your life and my life, side by side but not interfering with each other's, you never really learn what life is all about.

"In a good marriage, you borrow from each other your whole life long. If you're well matched, you've got what the other hasn't, and your partner's got what you need." She smiled again, a real smile that came from intimate knowledge of her subject. "But you got to know what to do with it. You got to get it all mixed up together, you got to not hold back, and not count turns, and you know what? It'll rise for you and grow like you wouldn't believe."

Could it be that simple?

Derek shifted in his chair. "I move fast. She likes to stop and examine every little thing. When I do that with her..." He hesitated, frustrated with the difficulty of explaining how it felt. "I get caught in the softness," he finally blurted. "I'm not sure I can ever be that way."

Babs nodded as though she understood. "I know. But you gotta give to get. It's a law of nature. Unless you're Trey Prentiss...." She made a face that told him what she thought. "And I can't think of one thing about him that's preferable to taking a chance."

Derek looked back at her, feeling a little as though he'd climbed the Himalayas and consulted the resident wiseman—or wisewoman.

He stood, leaned over her and kissed her cheek. He had a legendary reputation as a chance taker. Now was the time to live the legend.

"Thank you, Babs," he said.

She winked at him. "Sure. Hey, and if it doesn't work out, let me know. I've been looking for a younger man."

Chapter Twelve

"I don't know what to do," Kendra said, curled up in the guest house's rocking chair. "I've never had to consider anyone but myself before. I want to do the right thing."

Charlotte, holding the information Briane had learned, made herself sit quietly and listen.

"But..." Kendra sighed. "I don't know what that is."

When Charlotte offered no advice, Kendra glanced at her watch and gave her a grim smile. "Could you offer a pearl of wisdom, please? In just under an hour this place is going to be overrun with people expecting to attend a wedding." Her smile widened. "Remember what that's like?"

Charlotte laughed softly, unable to believe that just a matter of days ago the memory of her thwarted wedding still had the ability to hurt her. Had life changed that much in the past five days? Or had she changed.

"What's in your heart?" Charlotte asked. "What does instinct say?"

"Run as far away from this as you can get," Kendra replied instantly. "I just don't know if that's a healthy sense of self-preservation talking, or selfishness. Trey has hurt and embarrassed me, so it would be satisfying to show him that I can just walk away and make *him* look silly. It's tempting, but it's small. I want to be big in spirit. Like you are."

Charlotte blinked. "Excuse me? Big in spirit? Me? I was just going to vote for your plan to leave *him* at the altar."

Kendra smiled, then grew serious. "You are big. You built your own business. You came to help me even though I was engaged to the man who left you at the altar. You went above and beyond the call of duty with every little detail. You even interrupted your *honeymoon* to..."

"Stop!" Charlotte said, unable to bear another moment. When Kendra complied, wide-eyed at her unexpected shout, she added more quietly, "Stop, Kendra. That isn't true."

"It most certainly..."

"The part about my honeymoon." She sighed and let the burden slide off her shoulders. "Derek and I aren't married."

For a moment, the atmosphere inside the little guest house, as well as outside in the gardens, seemed to be absolutely still. There wasn't a sound or a movement.

Then Kendra asked quietly, "You're not? I don't understand."

Charlotte reminded her of the afternoon of her shower. "You know how our mothers have always...sort of...competed?"

Kendra nodded. "If that's what it's called."

"Caroline thought your mother was needling me because you had my old fiancé and I was still a single woman with nothing going for me, to her way of thinking. I think she's always disliked me."

Kendra frowned but didn't deny it. "I used to wonder about that. I think it's because you've always had more potential than I did. All I could do was look good in my clothes and sketch things. You were smarter and more serene. She resented you for it."

Charlotte shook her head over the injustice of a talent denied. "You have all the potential in the world. She just tried to make you another her rather than who you are. Anyway." She dismissed the philosophy with a wave of her hand. "Caroline came to my rescue with this announcement that I *was* married, supposedly to save me embarrassment." She laughed resignedly. "I can't tell you the trouble it's caused. So. If I am big, it's as a liar."

Kendra suddenly looked more interested in Charlotte's problem than her own. "You mean you and Derek have been sharing this guest house and you're not...?"

"No."

Kendra surprised her by laughing. "Well, that's hardly shocking in this day and age. But I can't imagine living in close contact with a gorgeous hunk like that and coming out with my libido intact."

Charlotte glanced at her, then snatched the throw pillow beside her and became interested in the ruffle surrounding it. "It isn't," she admitted. "I fell in love with him."

Kendra frowned in puzzlement. "That's good, isn't it?"

"No." Charlotte played with the decorative stitching. "I blew it. Things got serious, he got this frightened look in his eye, and I climbed all over him for it and told him it was over because it reminded me of Trey."

"Where is he?"

"His things are gone. I imagine he is, too."

"Charlie." Kendra disentangled herself from the chair and went to sit beside her. "You sound like you want him back. Shouldn't you be going after him?"

She swallowed a pointed lump in her throat and shook her head. "No. I'm beginning to believe I'm just supposed to plan weddings, not be in them. But the wedding at issue here is yours."

Remembering Briane's revelation in the garden, she said carefully, "Think hard, Kendra. Are you sure Trey's mind will stay changed? I know you love him, but if he marries you because..." She searched her mind for a plausible suggestion that wouldn't reveal what she knew. "Because he feels guilty for hurting you, or because he feels loyalty to your father, that wouldn't be good for either of you."

Kendra nodded, letting her eyes close for a moment. When she opened them, Charlotte saw again how much she'd changed in the past twenty-four hours.

"I know. But I was all ready to buy a house, have babies, set up a life the way I want to have it."

Charlotte could relate. She'd given that a little thought herself in the past few days. "But none of that would be any good with...with the wrong man."

"Trey told me to try to forget our conversation yesterday morning had ever happened. He said he just got a little panicky." She gave Charlotte a surprisingly whimsical smile given the subject under discussion. "He tends to do that, doesn't he? But he told me he loved me, begged me to forgive him and to marry him just as though the past day never happened. He seemed so sincere."

She shouldn't be the one to tell her, Charlotte thought desperately. It would sound vindictive and cruel coming from her. Then she decided that the real cruelty would be letting her marry Trey without knowing all the facts.

"Kendra..." she began.

A loud rap at the door interrupted her. Kendra peered through the drapes, then stood.

"It's my father," she said, smiling at Charlotte over her shoulder as she went to the door. "I guess it's time for me to make a decision."

"But, Kendra..."

"Hi, Kennie." Caleb wrapped his daughter in his arms, then smiled over her shoulder at Charlotte. "I'm sorry to break this up, but it's getting late."

Charlotte simply couldn't make herself say what she had to say in front of Caleb. *Kendra, you should know that your fiancé was bought for you by your mother.*

I'm sorry to tell you, Caleb, that you're married to a woman who values her social position above her daughter. Smile for Bitsy.

"Thank you, Charlie." Kendra reached out to squeeze her hand, then walked down the lane with her father toward the big house and very probably a miserable future.

CHARLOTTE PULLED her suitcase out from under the bed and opened her lingerie drawer. She smiled over the bittersweet memory of having done this once before. Then she felt choked with tears when she realized there was no one around to stop her this time.

She gallantly folded things into her suitcase, then into her garment bag, leaving out the high-necked, long-cuffed Victorian white lace she'd brought to wear to the wedding. She said a silent prayer that Trey would be struck by lightning and zapped into a responsible and faithful husband.

DEREK WAS HEADING for the lane to the guest house when Edward intercepted him at a remarkably agile run, the portable phone in his hand.

"Derek, I need you," he said urgently.

"But I . . ." He pointed to the guest house where he was sure Charlotte was probably packing, ready to escape the moment the ceremony was over. The rumor in the kitchen was that the wedding was going ahead as planned.

At the other end of the estate, guests were beginning to arrive. There was a stream of cars coming from the gate, and he could see Henry and Naldo moving among them.

Edward handed him the phone. "It's London."

"But you're..."

"I know. But he says he likes your style. He wants to talk to you."

He looked toward the guest house, then back to the phone in his hand. For the first time in his career he was willing to let a multibillion-dollar deal dangle in the interest of his personal life.

He was about to hand the phone back, to tell Edward he had to speak to his daughter, when he looked up again and saw Charlie moving across the lawn, a slender vision in white, hair piled high and haloed with flowers. Briane and Denise were with her, talking earnestly, as they made their way toward the tents, the plum and purple of their dresses a warm contrast to her white.

Derek groaned his resignation. The talk would have to wait. He exchanged a frustrated look with Edward, then put the phone to his ear.

"MAYBE IF WE all told her together," Briane said as she, Charlotte and Denise fought their way past caterers streaming outdoors to the shadowy interior of the house.

"Now?" Denise whispered harshly, tapping the little diamond-studded basal of her watch. "Ten minutes before the ceremony? *You* should have told her this morning."

"I tried, but she's been with her parents for the past forty-five minutes. Now she's getting dressed."

Charlotte remembered seeing the change in Kendra's eyes from the young woman she'd been two days ago to the woman she was this morning. She'd gotten a glimpse of the real Trey. Charlotte had to believe she had reached the decision she wanted to make, the one she could best live with—whether or not it conformed with what anyone else would have done.

Elizabeth shouted from somewhere upstairs. "Briane! Denise!"

With a parting look for Charlotte that expressed their common concern, they hurried upstairs in a flurry of taffeta and tulle.

Charlotte went to the French doors beyond which men, women and children in Sunday dress took their places in the hundreds of chairs placed on the lawn.

Caroline and Edward were greeting guests and sending them on to the ushers, who urged them into the rows of chairs.

A clear image of last year at this time rose in her mind, curiously unaccompanied by pain. All she felt was a deep gratitude for the way things had turned out—up until about a week ago.

Now pain did grasp her—biting and hard. Derek was gone, and it was all her fault. She imagined this was what happened to people who judged too harshly—they ended up alone.

She squared her shoulders and prepared to slide the doors aside. Everyone would look at her. She was the tragic figure, the woman who was always the bride's assistant, never the bride.

Ah, well. If loving Derek had taught her anything, it was that she did have a taste for the daring.

She pushed the door open and prepared to step out, but was halted by the touch of a firm hand on her shoulder. She spun around with a gasp of surprise and looked up into Derek's dark eyes.

"Derek!" she whispered, sunshine bursting inside her at the sight of him. "I thought you'd left."

"Did you?" He pulled her inside and reached past her to slide the French doors closed. "Just goes to show you how wrong you can be about a lot of things."

"Yeah, well," she said, her calm composure of a moment ago dissolving under his direct gaze. He'd changed into a suit, and the white of his shirt against the dark wool blend of his jacket gave him that mysterious edge of intrigue, like a portrait in black-and-white. "I...wanted to...talk to you about last night."

"Good." He took her arm and pulled her with him. "I have a few things to say to you, too."

There were staff everywhere, coming and going with food, chairs, last-minute adjustments to flowers and decor. Derek finally opened a door through which no one had entered or exited in the past few seconds and pushed Charlotte inside.

It was a pantry. Some recent visitor had left the overhead fluorescent on.

Derek closed the door behind them and kicked a step stool up against it to prevent intrusion. Then he turned to Charlotte.

Something in his eyes alarmed her. They were dark and bright and filled with a resolve that did not look entirely civilized. She backed away, past shelves of canned and boxed goods. He followed.

"I'm sorry I shouted at you," she said. "I hadn't reasoned out that feeling fear and acting on it are two different things. I just saw you looking frightened and that frightened me because..." She had to stop and swallow because he was still coming and she was now backed up against a shelf of onions and potatoes. A string of garlic hung above her head. "Because...I loved you so much. I think..."

He opened the buttons on his jacket and put a hand to the shelf above her head, blocking her in place. She edged sideways, and he reached his other hand up to a shelf of canned smoked oysters.

It was obvious she wasn't going anywhere. She had no other recourse but to admit the truth.

"I think I got so upset," she admitted, flattening herself against the mesh bags, turning her face sideways to avoid the look in his eyes on the chance that he didn't care, that he hadn't left simply because he didn't want to miss the opportunity to tell her what a pampered society brat she was. She swallowed again and closed her eyes. "Because I really wanted to have the wedding this time, and everything that comes after. The house, the kids, the pets, the van full of picnic stuff and Little League gear and car seats..."

He cupped her chin between his thumb and forefinger and turned her face to him. She opened her eyes. The emotion in his was so complex she couldn't read it.

"You want to know what I say to that?" he demanded.

The question had an edge of anger. Oh, God. This was it.

Without waiting for a yes or no, he lowered his head and opened his mouth over hers.

Derek let it all speak for him, the passion he'd always felt for her, steaming hot now because he'd come so close to losing her, the tenderness she'd taught him, the deep-rooted, far-reaching love that had grown so fast but felt as solid to him as the legs on which he walked.

As he kissed her lengthily, reaching deep with his tongue one moment, then lightly nibbling at her the next because his feelings were so entangled, so mercurial, he poured everything he knew about them at that moment into her. He loved her, he trusted her, he needed her, he wanted her. He would love her in return, never give her reason to doubt him for an instant, be there whenever she turned to him—during the daily struggle, and at night in their bed.

He raised his head and saw the tears on her face and the consummate happiness in her eyes.

"And furthermore," he said, his voice thick with emotion. He had so much more to tell her, but in the light of love in her eyes, words failed him. So he fell back on the language that had translated so well an instant ago.

The rattling of the doorknob finally drew them slowly apart.

"It can't be locked," a male voice said from the other side of the door. "There isn't a lock on it."

"Well, you try it then," an indignant female voice said. "Something's blocking the door."

Derek looked around them at the mundane contents of the kitchen pantry, then leaned down to kiss Charlotte's forehead and laugh lightly. "You won't be able to boast about the romantic nature of my proposal to our grandchildren."

Her arms, already wrapped around his waist, hugged him fiercely. "Romance is where you find it, in a Victorian loft or among the spuds and garlic."

He kissed the top of her head. "Then will you marry me, Charlie?"

"Yes, Derek," she replied, looking up at him, her eyes brimming with joy and promise. "The moment we get this one under way, we can plan our own."

"Then we'd better get out of here."

"Just one more kiss."

The pantry door burst open, the step stool scraping the floor as the spindly caterer and Pauline fell into the narrow enclosure. Derek, politely excusing himself, slipped past them, tugging Charlotte after him.

"Thieves?" the caterer asked Pauline.

The cook smiled fondly after them. "Lovers," she corrected.

CHARLOTTE AND DEREK saw Trey and his brother, who was serving as best man, standing at the French doors, awaiting the signal to go out onto the lawn to await the bride. They talked quietly together as Char-

lotte and Derek approached, Trey looking composed
and in control.

"A Beamer?" Trey's brother was saying, unaware
that he could be heard. "Or a Porsche like Cabot's?
That's a car."

"I think I'll get a plane," Trey said, smiling as he
speculated. "One of those new 31A jobs from Lear.
Has the best autopilot, flight director, panel layout and
nosewheel steering system of any Learjet airplane."

"You can't fly a plane."

"I'll hire a pilot."

"It'd be cheaper to fly commercially."

"But not as cool. Charlie! Cabot." Trey smiled with
great good humor as he slid the door open for them.
"Enjoy the wedding. Thanks for bringing my bride
home."

"Sure," Charlotte replied, barely resisting the urge
to kick him in the shin—or elsewhere. "Didn't want
her to be late for the delivery."

Trey raised an eyebrow. Derek frowned down at her.

"Delivery?" Trey asked.

Charlotte pretended confusion. "I have that wrong,
don't I? You're the one who was delivered, bought and
paid for by the magic formula that takes all the fear
away."

Trey went crimson to his hairline, like a glass filling
with claret. He glanced at his brother, who looked
confused, then back at Charlotte with a look of pleading.

"You didn't . . ."

"No, I didn't tell her," she said, making a sudden decision. Now that she knew what real love felt like, she couldn't let Kendra settle for anything less without making her see things as they were. "But I think I'll wait right here while you do. I imagine she'll be down any minute."

"I can expl—"

Charlotte stopped him with a raised hand. "Please don't try."

"You want to tell *me* what's going on?" Derek asked.

"Now *there's* a question." Bitsy Tate slipped in through the French doors Trey had opened, then slid them behind her. She looked up at Derek, a smug smile in place.

"You have *not* been to Massachusetts in the past four weeks," she said. "There is no health certificate or marriage license on file in any of the common-wealth's fourteen counties. You're going to pay for making me waste that time."

"You did it yourself, Bitsy," he replied reasonably, unable to dredge up even a vague ire over the revelation that seemed imminent. Being unveiled as a liar and, to some extent, a fake seemed a small price to pay for gaining Charlotte for a lifetime. "You could have just believed us and saved yourself a lot of trouble."

"But you lied," she said self-righteously, "and my job is to print the truth."

"Your job," he corrected, "is to ferret out every juicy little suggestion of scandal, every tender, spicy morsel you know your readers will digest with their orange juice." He smiled affably. "You wouldn't know the truth unless it was embroidered with lies and illicit suggestions."

Bitsy opened her mouth to retaliate, her fine-boned face going white and then purple. She closed her mouth and said coolly, "You two aren't married, are you? The lovely Victorian miss and the very contemporary hunk have been living in sin in the little guest house."

He raised an eyebrow. Her scornful glance at Charlotte finally activated his temper. "Do you really think anyone will care?"

She smiled slowly. "Of course they will. I'm sure they'd love to know that beautiful Charlotte Morreaux isn't married *this* time, either."

Charlotte caught Derek's arm as he took a step toward the reporter.

"It seems to me," Trey said calmly, "that this presents us with a new opportunity to come to terms, Charlie." He looked out at the large crowd of people waiting for the wedding to begin. Many of them had been at her almost-wedding. She knew in their hearts they'd probably sympathized with her position, but they'd eagerly gossiped about it for days anyway. She'd found it unsettling then to know that any given hour of the day someone was discussing her failed love life and her humiliation.

Curiously that didn't seem to matter now.

She smiled up at Derek. "Do you care?"

"Not a damn," he replied, "but you . . ."

"Don't give a damn, either. Trey Prentiss, you are such a lowlife they should make a place for you beside the escargots. And Kendra should know that. Then you are welcome to walk out there with Bitsy and announce our depravity to the world.''

The conversation was arrested by the beginning strains of "The Wedding March." Then there was the sound of a door closing upstairs.

"Well. That's us." Trey grinned at his brother, then winked at Charlotte. "Better think twice, Charlie." And he walked out, followed by his best man, to take his place beside the nearest trellis arch.

The atmosphere was heavy with tension, the music beyond the French door growing insistent. Happy for the diversion, Charlotte, Derek and Bitsy turned to watch the bride descend.

Chapter Thirteen

Everyone took a step back in surprise as Elizabeth appeared at the top of the stairs, a handkerchief pressed to her lips. She came down slowly, a feverish but unfocused look on her face, one hand clutching the hanky, the other hand on the gleaming mahogany banister steadying her progress.

Her beaded lavender jacket over a slim skirt flattered her figure, but lent a curious color to a face gone almost green.

"Elizabeth?" Bitsy asked, following her a few steps and getting no sign that she'd been heard or seen. "Elizabeth, what is it?" Elizabeth walked on as though in a trance.

"You may as well get it from me, Bitsy," Kendra said, appearing at the top of the stairs.

Everyone stared. It was easy to presume what had upset Elizabeth. Kendra was not wearing the white Victorian pinafore dress that had begun this whole charade. She wore a bright yellow suit and carried a tote bag. She was obviously dressed for traveling.

Caleb followed her down the stairs, carrying the rest of her bags.

Outside, the strains of "The Wedding March" continued to play in counterpoint to the little drama unfolding in the rear foyer.

Out of the corner of her eye, Charlotte saw Trey, straining to see into the house. But she was too pleasantly surprised to enjoy his concern.

"I'm not getting married today, Bitsy," Kendra announced calmly. Charlotte could see evidence that she'd been crying, but judging by the resolve in her manner, some decision about her future had permanently replaced the tears.

"The story's really too sordid for your column," Kendra went on, "although you could get Mother's version from her. I really don't care. I'll be touring Europe."

Bitsy looked a little avid, as though unable to wait to get to her laptop.

Kendra turned to Charlotte. "I heard you refuse Trey's offer to be silent." She hugged her. "Thank you. Dad had just told me the truth."

Caleb set her bags on the floor and shook his head grimly. "I didn't even know what Elizabeth had done until we got into a quarrel when you brought Kennie home this morning."

Kendra wandered to the door where the crowd was beginning to grow restless.

"I think we have to give them *something*," she said over her shoulder, a smile playing at her lips. "This could turn ugly if we don't handle it correctly."

"What do you have in mind?" Bitsy asked.

Without replying, Kendra slid the glass door open and beckoned to Trey, who was now looking decidedly uncomfortable.

The music stopped abruptly. He sent a quick glance at his brother, one at the crowd, gave them his endearing, apologetic smile, then loped across the lawn to the French doors.

"Kendra!" he gasped as he slipped inside. "What are you doing in that suit? Why..."

She stopped him with a very dignified but very final, "Trey, please. I know everything." She studied him a moment, as though looking for some sign in him of the man she'd loved, then sighed, apparently prepared to accept the truth that he'd never existed. "The kindest thing I can do for you at this moment is allow you to escape with some modicum of dignity. My father will explain to your family."

Trey looked around the little group in disbelief, that innocent surprise still in place on his perfect features. "Kendra, you misun—"

"Or," she suggested with a smile, "I could have Derek and my father escort you out."

The French doors slid open and Trey's brother looked Kendra up and down in her suit, then studied the hostile faces on the rest of the group and frowned at his brother.

"Is it off?" he asked.

Trey's answer was to stalk off in the direction of the front door. After a moment's hesitation, his brother followed.

Kendra dusted her hands, that unhappy task taken care of. Then she turned to Charlotte and Derek.

"I know just what'll save the day."

Charlotte, bursting with pride for her, hadn't a clue what she was talking about. "What?"

"Do you know that they *aren't* married?" Bitsy asked, "that they've tricked you and your family and everyone out there who was at the shower and who read my column?"

Kendra dismissed her with a swish of her lustrous blond hair. "Of course, I knew."

"You—?"

"I knew," Kendra repeated, then approached Bitsy with the same smile she'd given Trey. The older woman looked back at her warily. "But I wouldn't like to read it in your column. In fact, if you're tempted to write it, anyway, or to reveal the grisly details about Trey my mother will probably tell you, you might recall the night we went to the Karaoke bar."

"The bar?"

"Yes. You don't remember the second half of the evening, do you?"

"I...I..."

"If you recall, Briane was photographing the evening." Kendra put a companionable arm around Bitsy's shoulders and walked her a few steps in the direction Trey had taken. "I have photographs of you onstage doing a most interpretive version of 'After the Loving' with the drummer."

Bitsy made a little choking sound.

"And you were wearing your Saturday panties on Thursday. I'm sure the *Herald* could do a lot with that." Kendra smiled again. "Do we understand each other?"

Bitsy could only stare.

Kendra gave her a squeeze. "Good. Thanks for coming." She pushed her gently toward the front door.

She turned back to Derek and Charlotte and Caleb. "Now where was I?"

Caleb gave her a bear hug. "God. I didn't even suspect what you were made of, girl. You were about to save the day."

"Oh, right." She pushed the French doors wide, everyone in the chairs sat straighter and strained to see. She slipped one arm in Charlotte's and the other in Derek's. "Follow us, Daddy. We're going to need you."

"I'll be right behind you."

The orchestra struck up. "The Wedding March" one more time. She silenced them with a wave of her hand.

"Let me do the talking," she said, leading them toward the trellis arch, smiling at the hundreds of guests.

That was easy to agree to, Charlotte thought. If what she thought was about to happen was truly about to happen, she wasn't sure she could speak, anyway.

Kendra stopped before the stunned minister, still smiling. She stepped out from between Charlotte and Derek, then pushed them together until they were arm in arm.

"There," she whispered with satisfaction. "Don't you love it when things work out right." Then she faced her guests and cleared her throat.

"You've probably guessed by the way I'm dressed," she said, "that I'm not getting married today."

The low murmur that had greeted their walk to the trellis arch turned into a strengthening roar. She waited until it subsided.

"I apologize for keeping you waiting like this, and for the change in plans. Trey and I have had a change of heart," she said graciously, "but my parents had planned a lovely afternoon for you, and I'd like you to enjoy it, anyway. Toward that end, I've enlisted the help of Derek and Charlotte Cabot." She slanted them a wink that encouraged them to stay with her.

"Since they sneaked off to get married without us, I thought it only fair that they renew their vows today, since we have everything else in place."

There was a smattering of applause. Leading it were Caroline and Edward in the front row of chairs.

"Good. I'm glad you agree." She turned to her father. "Daddy, will you be best man for Derek?"

Caleb nodded with a smile. "I'd be honored."

She turned to beckon Edward, then Briane and Denise, who'd been waiting at the other end of the lawn for the bride to appear. They ran up the aisle to take their place behind Charlotte while Edward stood beside Caleb.

"But I don't have the renewal ceremony with me," the minister whispered in concern. "It isn't the same as..."

"Just do the wedding one," Kendra whispered back. "No one will know the difference."

Everyone on the lawn fell silent. The only sound was the drone of bees and the very small sigh of a breeze.

For an instant, her face sobered and she looked unutterably sad. Then she shook off the mood and said with satisfaction, "There." Then she hugged her father and turned for the house, shoulders square, step even.

The minister cued the orchestra and, once again, they struck up "The Wedding March." Charlotte saw the poetic irony in it as Kendra marched away to the melody.

Then, certain Kendra didn't require another moment's concern on her part, Charlotte turned her attention to the minister as he began the wedding ceremony.

She glanced up at Derek, who smiled down at her with an intimacy that made her feel as though they stood alone together despite their considerable audience. Everything inside her brightened and intensified.

She knew it was visible in her eyes—the rightness of this—Charlotte and Derek, the Duchess of Winter and the man who'd brought the thaw.

Derek felt swallowed in her gaze, welcome, caressed, shown the truth of everything she believed. *I am yours,* she told him silently, *and you are mine. From this day forward. Forever.*

He lost the thread of the minister's words for a moment and leaned down to kiss her with all the sweetness he'd learned in her arms, to let her know that she could expect it, that there would never be anything they couldn't share as she'd once thought.

"Ahem." The minister cleared his throat, glanced surreptitiously over their heads at the smiling audience and said under his breath. "That comes later. Pay attention."

He continued the ceremony, having to ask their names when they reached the vows. They spoke them so loudly and clearly that most of the audience thought the conviction in their voices came from having done this before so recently.

He finally pronounced them husband and wife, and Charlotte turned into Derek's arms. The afternoon breeze billowed the lace of her skirt, and fluttered the lock of dark hair on Derek's forehead.

A bird sang, the guests applauded and she could hear Caroline crying. Sunlight streamed on them through the latticed arch. She'd have been shocked had anyone pointed out to her that she was more aware of the reality of the moment than the romance.

Derek saw the breeze flutter a tendril of her hair and the baby's breath caught in it, saw the sunlight silver her eyes, so filled with love, and thought he would never forget the romance of their wedding day.

She pulled his head down to her and whispered, smiling, "Only a romantic would have done this, Derek. I've converted you, haven't I?"

He looked deeply into her eyes, love so strong inside him it was almost pain.

"The thing is," he whispered, "with us, romance is reality."

Epilogue

"I look like a truck wearing black stockings." Charlotte stepped back from the mirror in the hope that lengthening her reflection would slenderize it.

Derek walked behind her, affixing jade cuff links to his dress shirt, and stopped to evaluate her criticism. She wore a black crepe tent dress and black shoes with a low wedge heel. Pinned to her shoulder was the Victorian gold-and-enamel heart-shaped brooch he'd given her when she'd told him she was carrying their child.

She'd cut her hair short, a decision they'd argued over and he'd thought he'd won—until she came home with it cropped to her chin.

For a moment he'd been horrified. So many of the wondrous moments of his life had been spent all entangled in her hair. Then he'd seen the sparkle in her eyes, the beautiful definition of her chin and jaw, the graceful exposure of her neck, and he'd had to admit that he liked it.

Today he thought he'd never seen a more delectable, exciting woman in his whole life. He wrapped his arms around her and pulled her back against him to tell her so.

"You do not look like a truck. You look like a woman eight months' pregnant."

"I look like a truck eight months' pregnant." She waddled off to the bathroom. "I'm not going."

He didn't panic. After a year and a half as her husband, he knew how to deal with this mood. He tucked his shirt into his pants and fastened on the elasticized bow tie. "What do you want me to tell everyone?"

"The truth," she called, now out of sight.

"That you're feeling too fat to be seen in public?"

She came to the doorway, her shoes off, a lipstick in her hand. She frowned. "I'm sure you could put it more diplomatically than that."

He shrugged into his formal jacket, looking at her reflection just above his shoulder in the mirror.

"Kendra," he rehearsed, "I'm so sorry, Charlotte couldn't come to the opening of Paris Tout Partout, even though she promised when we bumped into you on our honeymoon that if you went to work and put a collection together she'd get all her friends to come and buy. She likes to look perfect, you know, like a genuine Victorian, and now that she's carrying my son, she doesn't like to be seen looking less than svelte." He paused to add significantly as he buttoned one button. "Even though she looks more beautiful than I've ever seen her."

She padded toward him in her stocking feet. "I did get a lot of people to come."

"You think they'll be as confident about buying if you're not there?"

"We might not feel confident about buying. We still don't know if she's any good. The stuff just came off the plane this morning and was hung this afternoon."

He caught her reflection and asked quietly, "Is that the point?"

She wrapped her arms around his waist and leaned against him. He felt the mound of her stomach against the small of his back and wondered if there was a more delicious feeling in the whole world.

"You're sure I don't look ugly?" she asked.

He reached behind him to tug her around in front and into his arms.

"You look absolutely gorgeous," he said with complete sincerity. "And you promised me this evening. The Butler wedding took so much of your time I've hardly seen you this past month."

That had the predictable result. Using guilt against her was shameless, he knew, but she needed to relax, and he knew she'd do it for him before she did it for herself.

He enticed her further with a few gentle strokes in the middle of her back. He took advantage of the opportunity to nibble on her neck. "We'll spend some time at the show, buy something even if we don't like it, then stop at Spago's on the way home for a late dinner, and when we get home I'll give you my famous back rub before we go to bed."

He knew he'd won when he felt her sigh and rest her weight against him. "As I recall," she said dreamily, "it was one of your back rubs that turned me into a truck in the first place."

THE GALLERY WAS FILLED with Kendra's friends and family and all of Charlotte's conscripts. And judging by all the red Sold dots on the title boxes, no one would have to be bullied into buying.

Charlotte was not surprised. She stared open-mouthed at the impressive collection of French city and pastoral scenes.

She supposed the style might have been called impressionist, although what little she knew about it brought to mind pastels and subtlety and a looseness that suggested rather than portrayed line and form.

The latter quality fit, but these colors were primary and bold and evoked strong feeling. Mood seemed to predominate rather than atmosphere.

Kendra greeted them just inside the gallery. In a sleek red dress that clung lovingly to every line and stopped mid-thigh, her hair in an elegant French twist, she looked like a woman in love with and in charge of her destiny.

She squealed in delight over Charlotte's girth and wrapped her in a hug. Then she drew back to look at her.

"How dare you wear that dress," Charlotte said in laughing indignation, "when I can't even get Derek's sweatshirt over my stomach."

"She exaggerates," Derek said, kissing Kendra's cheek. "She's now using most of my upper-body wardrobe. How are you? You look wonderful."

"I *am* wonderful." She raised a hand above the crowd to beckon to someone across the room. "In fact, I was thinking just this morning that Trey Prentiss was the best thing to happen to both Charlotte and me."

At Derek's and Charlotte's raised eyebrows, she explained simply, "He brought you two together and was responsible for my going to Paris. Antoine! Over here!"

A man just Kendra's height with thick, wavy auburn hair and a bright red moustache and beard materialized out of the crowd to slip into her extended arm. She gave him a resounding kiss.

"Antoine, these are my friends, Derek and Charlotte Cabot. Remember I told you they had my wedding instead of me? Cabots, this is Antoine Badineau, the most gifted sculptor in all of Paris."

He reached a hand out to Charlotte, and then to Derek. "I am delighted to meet you," he said in charmingly accented English. "Only a friend of *la belle's* could decipher such a sentence. 'They had my wedding instead of me.'" He repeated with a shake of his head. "In any other circle but Kendra's—" the *r* rolled on his tongue deliciously as his eyes rolled toward her "—it would not make sense. But I understand. She has bent my reality."

As a newcomer joined their circle to claim Kendra's attention, Antoine pulled them aside.

"Have you seen the pieces in the anteroom?" he asked, leaning closer to be heard in the growing crush of people. At the shake of their heads, he led them toward the back of the gallery. The crowd and the din were thinner here. He swept a hand to encourage them inside. "I believe there is a portrait of the two of you here."

"A portr—?" Charlotte began to ask in surprise, but he, too, had been claimed by a guest. She turned back to the room and saw it immediately.

Derek was already moving toward it, a large canvas depicting a summer lawn and garden and rows of chairs and women in hats and men in light-colored suits.

Dominating the painting were the figures of a woman in a high-collared white dress with wispy flowers in her hair, and a man in a dark suit bent gently over her. A minister garbed for ceremony faced them.

Derek put an index finger to the title box beside it. "Charlotte's Wedding," he read.

Charlotte lost herself in the painting. She experienced a reprise of everything she'd felt at that moment—all the love and hope and promise, all the wonder that it had all turned out so beautifully, after all.

She turned to Derek, wanting to tell him what she felt, but she didn't have to—the same emotions stood out clearly in his eyes. He kissed her quickly, then left the room and reappeared with the gallery owner, who placed the Sold dot on the box.

When the owner left, they stood back arm in arm to study themselves.

Suddenly an arm came around each of them, and a short figure in a crocheted shawl over a brown shirtwaist peered between their shoulders.

"Babs!" Charlotte said, reaching back to draw her into the middle.

Babs inclined her head toward Charlotte's swollen stomach. "I see you finally remember your name."

"You bet."

"And you." She looked up at Derek. "You took my advice, didn't you? You borrowed the magic."

He shook his head as he squeezed her closer. "No, I think this time I own it."

HARLEQUIN®

A M E R I C A N ◆ R O M A N C E®

Meet four of the most mysterious, magical men...
when Harlequin American Romance brings you

MORE THAN MEN

Make a date with Jason Merrick...

...in the Bermuda Triangle! Jason's deep blue eyes
were as unfathomable as the seas he inhabited. His
mysterious gaze could mesmerize women, just as his
tantalizing voice lured the creatures of the ocean. But,
as scientist Geneva Kelsey wondered, was he really
Jason Merrick... or Neptune himself?

Join Anne Marie Duquette for

#509   NEPTUNE'S BRIDE
November 1993

Don't miss any of the MORE THAN MEN titles.
Available wherever Harlequin books are sold.   SUPH-2

Harlequin is proud to present our best authors and their best books. Always the best for your reading pleasure!

Throughout 1993, Harlequin will bring you exciting books by some of the top names in contemporary romance!

In November, look for

BARBARA DELINSKY

First, Best and Only

Their passion burned even stronger....

CEO Marni Lange didn't have time for nonsense like photographs. The promotion department, however, insisted she was the perfect cover model for the launch of their new career-woman magazine. She couldn't argue with her own department. She should have.

The photographer was a man she'd prayed never to see again. Brian Webster had been her first— and best—lover. This time, could she play with fire without being burned?

Don't miss FIRST, BEST AND ONLY by Barbara Delinsky... wherever Harlequin books are sold.

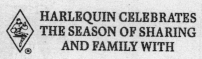

1993 Keepsake

CHRISTMAS

Stories

Capture the spirit and romance of Christmas with KEEPSAKE CHRISTMAS STORIES, a collection of three stories by favorite historical authors. The perfect Christmas gift!

Don't miss these heartwarming stories, available in November wherever Harlequin books are sold:

ONCE UPON A CHRISTMAS by Curtiss Ann Matlock
A FAIRYTALE SEASON by Marianne Willman
TIDINGS OF JOY by Victoria Pade

ADD A TOUCH OF ROMANCE TO YOUR HOLIDAY SEASON WITH KEEPSAKE CHRISTMAS STORIES!

HX93

Relive the romance...
Harlequin®is proud to bring you

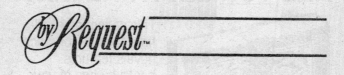

A new collection of three complete novels every
month. By the most requested authors, featuring
the most requested themes.

Available in October:

DREAMSCAPE

They're falling under a spell!
But is it love—or magic?

Three complete novels in one special collection:

GHOST OF A CHANCE by Jayne Ann Krentz
BEWITCHING HOUR by Anne Stuart
REMEMBER ME by Bobby Hutchinson

Available wherever Harlequin books are sold.